# THE EVE GENOME

## JOANNE BROTHWELL

The Eve Genome
Joanne Brothwell

ISBN-13: 978-1492760160
ISBN-10: 1492760161

Joanne Brothwell electronic publication: August 2013.
www.joannebrothwell.com

*The most robust statistical examination to date of our species' genetic links to 'mitochondrial Eve' – the maternal ancestor of all living humans— confirms that she lived about 200,000 years ago.*
*-Science Daily*

## CHAPTER ONE

ADRIANA SINCLAIR

Whenever I thought of my twin sister, Analiese, my mind predictably returned to the image of her scars. They were the kind of scars that screamed of her pain, an outer display of inner self-hatred. The healed skin was white and ropy, the way scars got after a long time, a latticework of pale spider webs that crept up her forearms. I hadn't seen her in a bathing suit in years, but I was certain if I did, I might see full words carved into the pale skin, maybe on her thighs on stomach. Words like *melancholy* or *misery* or *mourn*.

As a teenager I always wanted to ask her what those wounds felt like, on the inside. Not the physical pain of the exterior cuts, but the deep inner ache that would drive her to self-injury. As if once I knew what it was like, just how bad it truly was, I could take some of it away from her. But she never told me. She couldn't make the words come out of her mouth.

Was she afraid voicing the horror of what happened to her would bring it all back? A ghastly Technicolor flashback that would force her to relive it? Or was it because she couldn't bear to have me know? I'd suggested to her that talking to me about it might help, a way to release the trauma, but she couldn't. We'd gone twelve years of our lives sharing every little detail, and then, it all stopped.

I refocused on my current task, washing dishes. A final glass, one more fork, a bowl. I left them on the rack to air-dry. The apartment I was renting was mine alone—the stained beige carpet, orange pine cupboards, old vertical blinds and all. It was something I'd saved up for in my quest for freedom. Independence. I needed out, a place away from my childhood home, my mother. Away from Analiese. They had their emotional baggage and I couldn't be witness to the way that baggage weighed on them anymore. Living on my own was a lot harder than I'd expected, but despite the bills, the rowdy neighbours and the chronic leaky faucet, it was all worth it. I set the dishtowel on top of the sink full of clean dishes, went to the desk in my bedroom and fired up my laptop.

Tomorrow was the first week of college, my second year of unclassified studies. I had to choose a major within the next month or risk being kicked out. I barely knew what I wanted to do tonight or the next week, let alone the rest of my life.

The doorbell rang. I left my desk and pressed the talk

button on the intercom near the door.

"Who is it?" I asked.

"Adriana. It's Derek. Will you let me in?" It was Analiese's boyfriend. What in the world was he doing at my apartment?

"Okay." I pushed the button and the buzzer went off, followed by Derek's heavy footsteps as he bounded up the stairwell and entered the hall toward my apartment. I greeted him in the hallway.

"Hey. What's up?" I asked.

He stood in the doorway, an odd grin on his face. What was this?

"Can I come in?" Derek asked. I shrugged and opened the door. He walked into the apartment and the door shut automatically behind him.

He was suddenly right in front of my face.

"I've always wanted to try out the other twin," he said as he leaned into me, my back up against the wall. His muscular frame was taking up my entire field of view and his face was so close to mine I could feel the heat of his skin emanate onto my cheeks. His mouth curled up into a sexy half-smile, an expression that didn't reach his eyes.

Six months ago I'd wanted to be with him so badly I couldn't help but share my infatuation with my twin sister, Analiese. Our relationship was strained, and I confided in her with the hope of reconnecting over a topic I thought was neutral territory for us both. A crush. I wouldn't have predicted what she did following my admission. I never expected her to seduce him.

"What do you think, hun?" Derek asked with a wink. I used to think he was one of the most gorgeous guys I'd ever met, with dark brown hair and powder-blue eyes that always made my heart pound. Before, I would have thought he was charming; his flirtation, flattering. But now, he was my sister's player boyfriend. Was I going to become my sister's betraying twin?

"Why did you come here?" I asked. I'd never had Derek in my apartment before tonight. He was way too big for the space.

"Analiese told me. She said you were hot for me, before we started dating." Derek's lip twitched. "And I had to find out for myself. I came straight over."

The memory of Derek's hands splayed across Analiese's naked back in the dark interior of the camper that night seeped into my thoughts, unbidden. I had thought Derek was alone in the camper that night. I was wrong.

They didn't even notice when I'd walked in, probably because they were both... occupied. I'd stumbled out, and it wasn't because I was too drunk. The pain of learning what my own sister had intentionally done to me made my reality tilt. My body felt unhinged, as though I was a paper doll in a pulp world. All make-believe. All bad comic book garbage. Veronica fucks Betty over by messing around with Archie.

Derek swept a stray hair from my face with a deliberately

gentle touch, pulling me out of my dark memory and back into the present awkward moment. The moment of truth. Betty always gave in to Archie. Would I?

"Hey, you," he said. I shivered from the sensation of his hot breath on my skin. He smelled sweet and spicy, but with an artificial overtone. Like cinnamon hearts made with aspartame. "If only I'd known you were into me six months ago..." he trailed off.

This was the first time I'd ever been this near to Derek. There was a time when I'd yearned for this moment, dreamed of it, would have done anything to experience it. Here was my opportunity. But this was all wrong.

"Would things be different?" I asked.

His pupils dilated and he lowered his face even closer. "Definitely."

I looked up at him and did a double take. His eyes. They weren't powder blue like I'd always thought they were. Instead, his right eye had a strip of muddy brown dissecting the blue. Heterochromia, the genetic quirk that resulted in two distinct colors within the same iris.

He tipped my chin up, his thick arm between us. I glanced away. I needed space. Oxygen. His cotton t-shirt was fitted to his arms, a deliberate attempt to highlight thick biceps. A snake tattoo twisted from his wrist all the way to his upper arm, a forked tongue that eternally lashed out at his heart.

"What's wrong?" Derek asked. The timbre of his silky

voice made my stomach feel funny. Sour. He leaned down and whispered into my ear, "I want the other twin, Adriana. I want you." My body broke out in a rash of gooseflesh. His saccharine sweet aftershave coiled around me and my guts knotted up even more.

He was doing his best to charm me right out of my pants, but there was something about the way he spoke... something disingenuous, dirty. I'd heard the way he talked to Analiese. It was always with the utmost respect. He changed octaves for her, his voice lilting and breathy, as if he was telling her his deepest, innermost secrets. It sounded nothing like this.

I placed my open hand on Derek's chest and pushed him away. "Don't touch me." I took a definitive step to the side, ducking away to put enough space between us so his hand fell away from my face.

His mouth dropped open, as if he couldn't possibly comprehend what I'd just said or done. Was he really that much of a cocky bastard that he thought I'd just let my clothes melt off for him? Did he think I couldn't possibly withstand the power of his seduction that I would actually betray my twin sister for him? He held out his hands, palms up. I almost rolled my eyes at the brazen over-confidence.

"I thought you were in love with her."

"There's lots of love in my heart," Derek said with a wide grin. Looking at him now made my skin crawl. The oddness of his eyes, blue with a slash of sludge through the middle, made him seem so fickle he couldn't even stick to one simple eye color.

I glared at him and said, "I'm going to tell her."

The smile fell from his face in a flash. "What are you going to say? Hey, Analiese, your boyfriend wants me. That's right. He wants me 'cuz I'm the prettier twin." Derek's voice was high-pitched and snarky, like a back-talking adolescent. "Yeah, that will go over really well. I'm guessing she won't be thankful for the message. If she even believes you, which she won't. Don't forget, I'm the guy she fucks every night."

"You're an ass," I said. "Get out."

The lock in the front door clicked with the turn of a key and then opened. Analiese!

She stood there, her black hair pulled back into a ponytail, wearing running shorts and a tank top. The apples of her cheeks were flushed pink and the bright teal of her eyes smoldered within the surrounding circle of white. Her mouth hung agape as she took in the spectacle of her boyfriend, here, at my apartment.

"What the fuck...?" Analiese muttered.

"It's not what you think," Derek said.

Wasn't that the guiltiest thing a person could possibly say in a situation like this?

Analiese's eyes narrowed. "Then what is it, Derek? Adriana?" Her voice was low and far too quiet.

"He was hitting on me," I said, the words tumbling from

my mouth, making me sound way too guilty. "He's a player."

Analiese's stormy gaze came to rest on Derek. "Is that true?"

Derek laughed. "No." He looked back and forth between us, his lips opening and closing and his eyes flashing like an electric eel. "I was here to ask Adriana a question." His cheeks flushed red. "Adriana must have misunderstood why I was here. Geez. That's embarrassing for you."

"You liar," I said through gritted teeth. I grabbed Analiese's hand. "He's full of shit, Analiese. You know that, right?"

Analiese yanked her hand from mine. "Don't. Touch. Me." Her nostrils flared as she looked at me with an expression that could only be described as bewildering contempt. She spun on her heel and ran out the door, down the hall.

"Analiese, wait!" I called as I pulled my shoes on. She was now in the stairwell, footfalls pounding in a staggered pattern like she was going down two at a time. By the time I got out into the stairwell I could already hear Analiese's engine start up outside.

"Shit," Derek muttered.

"Get. Out!" I yelled back at Derek as I entered the stairwell. I ran down the steps and to the street, but she was already pulling away. The engine roared on her little VW Beetle, and a swell of dust billowed up behind it.

I stood, staring at her car as it disappeared from view. She'd obviously stopped by on her way home from the gym before we started our first semester tomorrow. She probably wanted to talk textbooks or syllabus or something. She definitely wouldn't have been expecting to see Derek in my apartment, his body hunched toward me like he was about to dry hump my hip. Fuck.

When she turned out of sight, I went back inside. Derek was putting his shoes on in the doorway.

"I'm sorry," he said.

I held the door open for him and glared.

Derek stepped out of my apartment. "Do you think she'll forgive us?"

I shut the door in his face, and turned the deadbolt.

Where the hell was my purse? I glanced around, my heart thumping an erratic beat. It was on the floor. I rifled through it, got my phone out and typed in a message.

*I need to talk to u*

Several minutes went by as I stared at the screen of my phone, willing it to show a response. There was nothing. I typed in her number. After six rings, it went to voicemail. I hung up.

Analiese would understand once I explained. She would hear me out. Once I told her it was all Derek, and I turned him down, she would know it wasn't me. He was a dumbass boyfriend, someone disposable. But I was her sister. Her blood. She would have to listen. She would have to hear me out.

I couldn't just sit and wait, so I grasped my purse and keys, left my apartment and got into my car. I pulled away, not knowing where to go. As if on autopilot, I drove toward my mother's house. Once on her street, I idled slowly by the front of my childhood home. Analiese's bug wasn't there. I turned to head down the back ally. No cars were parked behind the house. Obviously nobody was home. I left, wandering aimlessly, my mind spinning in circles, outpacing my erratic driving.

I drove for an entire hour before I finally gave up and returned home. Now it was dusk and everything was tinged a shade of blue as the sun receded, the light turning away from the world, leaving it cold, dark and alone. I shut off my engine and sat in my silent car.

A strange sensation folded over me, like a shroud of darkness that clouded my vision, choked out all oxygen in my lungs and settled deep in my bones like a malignant tumour. My heart skipped a beat. I'd had this feeling once before. When Analiese broke her arm at soccer in fifth grade. Something was terribly wrong.

Analiese.

My cell phone rang. I dug it out of my pocket, my hands shaking as I pressed it to my ear.

"Hello?"

My mother's voice came through the receiver, her voice shrill and digressive. "There's been in an accident. It's Analiese."

#

My knees buckled when the announcement came over the

Emergency Room intercom – *Trauma Team to Resuscitation Two.* They were talking about Analiese. I grasped the wall to steady myself as the doors to the ER flung open with my sister on a stretcher pushed by frowning paramedics, her body nearly obscured by the wires, tanks, and piles of bloody gauze around her.

They wheeled her straight into the trauma room. Others rushed in behind them and a woman in a surgical mask closed the door. I looked down. Droplets of Analiese's blood marred the white tile floor. Four round crimson circles, evenly spaced apart.

I watched them work on her through the windowpane in the door. Analiese's prone body was lit up by two huge overhead lamps. Part of her face was covered with a mask, and under that, a cervical collar. Her complexion was pallid, as if fine ash covered her skin. The intermittent whirr of oxygen tangled with the shrill beep of the heart monitor.

There were so many people around her. Like in an overwrought medical TV drama, they wore blue scrubs, some with huge plastic face visors and others in protective glasses and surgical masks. But this wasn't television. At the time, the phone call from my mother didn't seem real, but now, everything was in painfully sharp focus. Their movements were rapid and purposeful as they turned dials and grabbed supplies from the row of cabinets along the wall. A tray of barbaric steel instruments lay beside her examination table, tools that looked like medieval torture devices. The acidic stench of antiseptic burned up my nose. Someone brushed me aside and stepped through the door.

A female voice rang out. "Get lab down here for a type and cross-match."

"There's no time. Get O-neg," the doctor said, authority in his tone.

A blood transfusion? I took a deep breath, but it didn't help, only serving to make me feel even more breathless and out of control. Where was mom? Why hadn't she arrived yet? Why did this happen? Body trembling, knees like water, I leaned against the door for support.

"Hang in there, all right?" a female attendant said, her face tilted down to Analiese. Was she conscious? Were her eyes open, watching this spectacle, unable to move? Was she scared? I wanted to go to her, hold her hand and tell her everything would be okay, just like I did when we were kids.

A male voice spoke next, "There are going to be a few people working on you, now."

An alarm went off and the sound was like an electrical jolt through my body. Instantly, all movements sped up. The air in my lungs rushed out as if they were balloons deflated by the poke of a pin.

"Code blue. We have a code blue."

An unwanted image flashed through my mind. Of Analiese's cold, dead body, her skin bluish-gray, eyes glossy and rolled back in her head. I took a step forward, pushing the door ajar.

"I told you O-negative. What did you give her?" the doctor barked out.

"It was O-negative!"

A string of muttering followed. "She's rejecting it."

Another alarm sounded, one that droned on and on, flat and toneless. I stepped into the room, unnoticed by the harried staff inside.

"Her pressures are dropping," An edge took over the doctor's voice, raising the pitch. He leaned over and began compressions on Analiese's chest. Sweat broke out under my arms and my vision tunnelled. Every argument we'd ever had tumbled through my mind, one by one until our final conflict today. About Derek.

"AED ready," someone snapped.

My hearing hollowed and stars floated in my vision as the whine of the AED charged. The thump of the current through Analiese's chest made a shriek slip from my mouth. Compressions continued, and the process was repeated, over and over. Every time the electricity slammed through Analiese, I felt as if my own heart was about to stop.

All of the sounds died at once.

Nobody moved. Then little by little, the posture of each and every person around Analiese's hospital bed drooped. One by one, their hands fell to their sides.

I couldn't breathe.

"T.O.D. eight forty-one," the doctor said.

My body went ice-cold. I stepped backward, out of the room and turned to look down the long hallway, my muscles tightly coiled, shaking.

"Miss?" The ER doctor approached me with a steely gaze, mask pulled down, hanging limply around his neck, his visor pushed high on his head. He paused, mid-step, and then resumed walking towards me. His mouth was a tight, thin line. Like a slash made by a sharp scalpel. "I'm sorry. We did everything we could."

I tried to respond, but nothing would come out of my mouth. I felt like someone had punched a hole into my chest wall and ripped my heart out. Gutted. Like a pumpkin.

The doctor scratched the dark stubble on his chin. "Has she ever received blood products and had a negative reaction before?"

I shook my head, but my mouth remained locked.

"In twenty-three years of practicing medicine..." The doctor swallowed. "I have never seen anything like this before."

*Allele: An allele is an alternative form of a gene (one member of a pair) that is located at a specific position on a specific chromosome. These DNA codings determine distinct traits that can be passed on from parents to offspring.*
*-Biology.About*

## CHAPTER TWO

### ADRIANA SINCLAIR

I approached the medical lab, the huge metal letters *GenMed* glaring down from above the stark grey building. There were giant boxy mirrors every few feet, the effect like a giant, colorless Rubik's cube. Cold pragmatism.

I reached into my purse and my fingertips brushed against Analiese's yellow cotton t-shirt, the one she was wearing on our twelfth birthday, before everything between us went downhill. The fabric was soft, nearly sheer in places from years of wear. Her favorite shirt. Her lucky shirt. The one that helped her soccer team win the gold medal that season. The one she wore almost every day under her clothes to cover up and push down her new boobs. My matching shirt was long gone, but Analiese's was still intact, tucked away in her room at mom's house. I clutched the fabric tight and closed my eyes, squeezing against the permanent heat at the back of my eyes. An image of her, age twelve, in this exact shirt slid through my mind. She was carefree then, full of energy and ideas and plans for the future. Black hair flying in the wind, her wiry body would flit and jump and dance with all her exuberant energy. She would run up to me and do a pirouette a foot from my nose. *Maybe we could be rock stars, Adriana? Or maybe you could play guitar and sing and I'll play drums?* But that was Analiese before.

I opened my eyes and scanned the exterior of the building for the doorway. Both the building and the landscape around it were bleak, concrete and treeless, totally unlike most of Colorado. I'd never been in this part of Stonewood. Despite nineteen years here, I'd never seen this building. Analiese and I had never had a medical problem before. For the most part, Stonewood was like a big town in the middle of a picturesque countryside of behemoth mountain ranges and crystal clear lakes. The population was only one hundred fifty thousand, much of that made up by college students who repeatedly came at the start of the semester and left as soon as finals were written after second semester. The residents who remained were average people who went back and forth from home to work and back again. The crime rate was low and Analiese and I'd always felt safe living here. Now, everything was different. The stoic grey building bore down on me, as if I was being crushed by a vengeful mountain god.

Yesterday, my twin sister's life ended. For nineteen years we lived every day of our lives together, sharing each and every milestone. Each event was unalterably etched in my brain. Our first day of kindergarten wearing matching blue tights and navy dresses, our grade three performance when we got to play sisters in the school play, and our first day of college last year.

It wasn't all perfect. In fact, most of it after seventh grade was rough. Analiese was moody, temperamental, overly-sensitive. All because of Uncle Les. He destroyed her innocence, took it from her without so much as a blink. And after that, everything about Analiese changed, irrevocably. She looked different. She acted like a different person. Uncle Les didn't just steal her childhood. He broke her spirit.

I should have realized something was terribly wrong when, at fifteen, she pierced her own tongue, or when she spray painted the word HATE in huge black letters across the back of her jean jacket. I should have noticed something when she started smoking, and doing drugs. But I didn't. It took seeing the perfectly spaced cuts from her elbow to her wrist for me to realize how bad it was. And even then, I didn't realize the half of it. I knew she was angry, full of rage. But I didn't realize how much her anger and resentment was directed towards me. I became acutely aware that night, inside the camper, when she decided she wanted Derek, the boy I told her I had a huge crush on. After that, everything between us changed.

Now all that was left of her was an empty shell, a carcass that had once housed the most beautiful, damaged soul I'd ever known. One I almost betrayed on the day of her death. I wished it had been me that died that day.

I looked straight up, to the top of the building. If I could figure out a way to get onto the roof, I could... avoid all of this. Avoid these pushy medical people and their pushy recommendations. Avoid my mother's tortured expressions that belied her inner pain. Avoid *feeling*.

The same people who failed to save Analiese insisted I get my blood typed. Not only did they insist, but someone at the hospital even went to the effort of making me an appointment with the lab.

With a hollow chest, I stepped through the doorway into the building and was immediately greeted by a receptionist behind a brushed-metal desk. She wore a headset over a coiffed up-do of blond hair, and her French manicured nails tapped away at her computer keyboard. *Click-click, click-click.* When she saw me, she stopped.

"May I help you?" she asked. Her black eye makeup was drawn on to create a perfect set of cat-eyes.

"I'm here for genetic testing. My appointment is at ten thirty," I said.

The woman looked at her computer screen and clicked the mouse. *Click. Click. Click.* When she saw what she was looking for, she smiled at me, a closed-lipped, *you're wasting my time,* kind of smile. "Adriana Sinclair?" she asked. I nodded. She gestured to the waiting room. "You can have a seat." Her nails began their incessant tapping once again.

I glanced over at the glassed-in elevator on the side wall. I could probably be halfway to the top floor before the receptionist even noticed I'd walked away. Instead, I sat down in one of the black and chrome armchairs and rummaged through the stack of magazines beside me. I was too weak. Suicide would be too hard. I could barely get myself to brush my teeth properly right now, let alone muster up the energy to kill myself.

"Miss Sinclair?" someone asked. It was a woman in a lab coat, whose nametag hung off her pocket like a badge of honor. A nod to days gone by when status and prestige were marked by the amount of brass on your uniform. She wore sensible brown leather shoes that looked like a cross between loafers and hiking boots. Her brown, shoulder length hair was paired with plain, no-nonsense makeup. "You can follow me, please." I followed her to a room that looked and smelled much like a doctor's office, with sterile white walls, white cupboards, alcohol, tongue depressors and cotton balls on the countertop.

She gestured for me to take a seat. "I'm Dr. Dorlett. I understand hospital staff had some difficulty typing your sister's blood?" The doctor stared straight at me, her dark gaze unwavering, but I knew what she thought when she saw me. A barely-an-adult grownup wanna-be who'd lost her sister but who wasn't quite out of the denial phase yet.

"That's correct. My twin sister was killed by a blood transfusion. She was in a car accident." Even saying the words made my eyes well up with tears and my throat swell. My twin sister was killed. Would this become my new mantra? A phrase I'd repeat, over and over again, until I, the other twin, died too? *Twinkilled.*

Over the years it was a phrase I frequently thought about. How I would explain my sister's suicide. The years between fourteen and seventeen was a living hell as I was required to sleep with her, in her room, on suicide watch, twenty-four hours a day. Day in and day out I was responsible for keeping her alive. I'd grown twitchy and paranoid to leave her, afraid to take too long in the bathroom or take a nap. By the end of her depressive episode, when we were seventeen or so, I was so hyper-vigilant I actually started to see flashes of something black in my peripheral vision. Not hallucinations, my doctor said, just the manifestation of an overactive, overanxious brain.

It all started after that first trip to the hospital, Analiese dripping blood from her arms, her face white and stoic. My mother thought it was less intrusive if I was the one on suicide watch, since we were twins. Over time, I grew to resent them both.

I'd done it, watched over her, kept her alive and sacrificed my own mental health, almost to our twentieth birthday, all for it to be over in the blink of an eye. *Twinkilled.*

Dr. Dorlett flipped through a chart. Her eyes shadowed over and a crease formed in her forehead. I felt suddenly unsettled, as if the floor had just gone off-kilter and I was sliding, down, down, down, deep into the unknown. Purgatory.

Her navy blue eyes flicked up from the chart to me and back down again. "These lab results indicate they were unable to type your sister's blood at all." She stared at the document, her rutted brow and grooves around her mouth so deep her entire face looked harsh, like an antique marionette doll. "There must be an error."

I remained silent, not knowing whether she was asking me a question or not. When her penetrating eyes met mine once again, I felt all the more ill-at-ease.

"This is inaccurate." Doctor Dorlett's eyes were as cold as a storm-tossed sky. "The lab clearly made an error. Let's take a vial of your blood for typing and I'll call them to discuss the results."

I took a deep breath and closed my eyes as the doctor tied a band around my bicep and slid the needle into the vein at the crook of my elbow. I opened my eyes. The reddish-blue blood spurted into the tube with every beat of my heart. Three vials of blood filled before she removed the needle. She pressed a cotton ball to the puncture wound and left with the vials. I remained alone in the cold, sterile room. I pulled the cotton ball back and stared at the crimson round stain against the snowy white cotton fibres.

How could a hospital ER or lab make an error? Wasn't blood typing a common, routine practice? Weren't there only four or five blood types anyway? The whole situation stunk of negligence and people careful to cover their ass.

My bracelets rattled from my hands shaking. I pulled my cell phone out and surfed the internet for lawyers who specialized in medical malpractice. I clicked on the first one I saw, and pressed the dial button.

I sucked in a deep breath and let it hiss out, hoping to calm my vibrating body. Dr. Dorlett returned after only one ring into my phone call and handed me a piece of paper. I hung up.

The five-by-seven page had four circles across the top and blood spots in each of the circles. Beneath each circle had a title— Anti A, Anti B, Anti D and Control. My name was beneath all the circles.

"Do you see how each one of those droplets has little dots?" The doctor asked, her eyebrows high on her forehead. I nodded and she continued, "That means the test is invalid. One of them should look like a fully formed circle." Dr. Dorlett grasped three more of the same little papers from the chart. "So I repeated the process. Three times. All three times were invalid." She handed the other three papers to me and all of them looked exactly like the first. "These are the tests from the hospital lab that were performed on your sister's blood type."

I stared at the blood tests with Analiese's name on them.

All of them had that same spotty blood in the four circles.

I looked up at her. "What does this mean?"

"There was no mistake at the hospital. You and your sister's blood can't be typed." The doctor's face turned slightly pink.

"I don't understand."

Dr. Dorlett's mouth pinched together. "I'm sorry. I can't explain it any more than that. Our lab can't help you. I've referred you to The National Human Genome Research Institute and the Center for Inherited Disease Research. I understand this is where the Coroner has sent your sister's body for further examination."

A jolt shot through to my stomach. "What? They've sent Analiese somewhere without telling us?"

The doctor took the blood typing results from my hands and placed them back into the file. "I'm sorry. There's nothing more we can do for you here."

#

My mom, Carla picked me up and we wasted no time flying to Bethesda, Maryland, where The National Human Genome Research Institute was located. Once we touched down in Bethesda and retrieved our luggage, we hailed a cab, neither of us feeling emotionally capable of driving. Mom spent nearly the entire ride on her cell, contacting government officials, politicians and anyone else she could angrily scold and threaten with a lawsuit. It was all a pathetic attempt to distract herself from the horror of our situation. Her child was dead. Threatening people would provide a temporary relief, the sharp focus of anger a way to contain the ugly pain. But the grief would come back. There was no escape.

Before, mom had been only mildly unhappy with her life, thanks to my dad who had decided to turn everything upside down three years ago. She'd been busy focusing on her career as a real estate agent when my dad, Tom, up and left following a torrid affair. Mom was the embodiment of the saying, 'had the rug pulled out from under her feet'.

I stared out the window, noting the lush landscape of this coastal city, but unable to appreciate it. One dead tree among the green caught my eye, the whitened branches gnarled into a twisting spiral, reaching up to the heavens. In my peripheral vision, a snow-white jackrabbit sprang through the weedy ditch, bee-lining for the trees alongside the road. It watched our moving car with one round, crimson-red eye and then hopped off into the trees, disappearing from view.

I glanced at mom, her dark brown hair and pale skin seeming to amplify the worry lines below her eyes and around her mouth. She had her hair cut in a bob that normally was styled to look funky and cute, but today, with the way it hung in lank strips around her face, I wasn't sure she'd even combed it. I could hardly criticize. My own waist-length black hair hadn't been washed in three days and I'd kept it tied back in a messy ponytail the entire time.

Showering seemed to be a privilege, something only

worthy people were allowed to do, a form of self-care for deserving people only.

Analiese's death couldn't have happened at a worse time for mom. After my dad left, I knew at least mom had Analiese at home. But now, I was all my mom had left. Would my dad want to come to the institute as well? Would he try to sweep in like Disneyland daddy and participate in this mess? Grieve his dead daughter and pretend to support me? The last thing I wanted right now was to see the man who'd destroyed any and all self-esteem mom once had. Analiese and I hadn't spoken to him for over a year and a half. It was just easier that way.

We settled into our hotel, showered and got ready for our meeting scheduled later in the afternoon. When the time arrived for us to depart for the institute, I had butterflies in my stomach that felt more like jumping razorblades.

The National Human Genome Research Institute was made up of several large buildings, reminding me of a college campus. A pang of regret hit me. Would I even attend college after this? Would I de-enroll, give up my apartment, move in with mom and retreat into my bedroom? Retreat into myself? Studying seemed like such a privilege now. A privilege Analiese would never get. I didn't deserve it.

The tall main structure was a unique combination of red brick and shiny glass windows, giving it both a traditional and contemporary feel, a seamless blending of old and new. We got out of the cab and despite the sensation that my legs were encased in concrete, I pushed forward to the entrance.

Inside, we came to a large granite wall of financial donors. We approached the information desk off to the left and were greeted by a pretty Asian woman with prominent cheekbones, eyelash extensions that nearly reached her eyebrows and hair pulled back into a fancy up do. She appeared tiny behind the mammoth round desk that enclosed her.

"Welcome to NHGRI. Where can I direct you?" she asked.

"My daughter's body has been sent here for autopsy," Mom said.

"And I've been referred here by GenMed in Colorado," I added. My stomach growled but all three of us pretended not to hear. I'd totally forgotten to eat today. The woman peered at us with dark brown eyes, as if she knew precisely who we were. But that was hardly likely, wasn't it?

"Adriana Sinclair? Welcome. The research team is awaiting your arrival."

My belly tightened and my mouth went dry. A research team. Why would a research team be waiting to see me? Why, with the massive size of this institute, which probably employed hundreds of people, why would this one woman, clearly a receptionist, know I was coming? Because of the blood typing?

"Please, have a seat. I will let Dr. McGill know you're here." She motioned for us to take a seat along the wall. We sat down on the row of vinyl chairs beside a dove-grey bare wall, save for one huge, wall-spanning iridescent image of a 3-D double helix. Blue, green and red little balls all attached by spindles of grey that twisted from top right to the bottom left of the photo frame.

A small woman in a white overcoat with a weasel-y look approached us. When she spoke, her top lip came to a point. "Hello, I am Andrea, one of the postdoctoral students here at NGHRI. I'll escort you to the boardroom now. Please, follow me."

We followed her down a corridor to an elevator that took us up to the sixth floor. There, she led us past several science labs and into a boardroom. Inside was a large oak table with numerous people in lab coats already seated around it. In the middle were x-rays, paper documents and a chart. At one end of the room was a painting that took up two-thirds of the wall. It was four circles filled with concentric rings that looked vaguely like four evenly placed targets. The colours ranged from burgundy on the outer edge to pale pink on the inside. I couldn't stop staring at it.

A booming voice startled me from my fixation on the artwork. "Adriana and Carla Sinclair." The man stood at the head of the table, wearing a navy blue suite that seemed far too small for his tall, approximately six-foot-four frame. He had greying brown hair and a reddish-brown goatee. His John Lennon spectacles emphasized his froggy-round eyes, prominent nose and long two front teeth. "I'm Dr. McGill, Director of the Human Genome

Project. I'm terribly sorry to hear about Analiese." He strode toward us and thrust his hand out to mom, his coat sleeve riding up to reveal thick, curly forearm hair.

Mom took his hand and shook it, nodding and blinking fiercely, forcing back the tears. I looked away. Then Dr. McGill took my hand and shook it with a gorilla-firm grip. His palm was surprisingly warm.

"Thank you. Her loss has been devastating," Mom said, her voice choked.

"I'm sure it has been, Ms. Sinclair," he said. Somehow, his words and his manner seemed disingenuous. Like he was saying what he thought was appropriate for the situation, pacifying us until he could get to what he really wanted to talk about. "Please, have a seat. We need to speak to you about a number of our findings with respect to your daughter's genetic makeup."

Dr. McGill took a chair at the head of the table.

We sat closest to him, though I had no idea why, considering there were numerous chairs open elsewhere around the table. Dr. McGill proceeded to introduce everyone. All of the intros began with doctor and then their particular specialization, Dr. Jones, Genetic and Inherited Diseases; Dr. Bomer, Genetics and Molecular Biology; Dr. Halan, Genome Technology. There were nine scientists altogether, but after the fifth person, I stopped listening. They all sounded the same.

"There are some significant anomalies about Analiese's

genetics," Dr. McGill seemed to be choosing his words carefully. "Were you aware of this, Ms. Sinclair?"

"You can call me Carla." Mom said and then shook her head, her eyes wide. "Anomalies other than the blood type?"

"I suppose the most intriguing is the blood type. Genetically, her blood type is extremely rare, which explains her body's refusal of blood products."

I sat forward so fast the leather seat squeaked against my jeans. "Is there an explanation?" I asked.

"Occasionally, we see marked genetic differences such as this in individuals, and it is our job to investigate the anomaly, to determine if it is a genetic variant, a mutation of some kind, or if it is an inherited disease." Dr. McGill paused. "That's why Analiese's body has been brought here. For investigation."

"What does an investigation entail, exactly?" Mom asked.

Dr. McGill placed his hands on the file full of papers in front of him, his large, knobby fingers splayed so he was touching almost every page. "Before we get into that, I'd like to ask a few other questions about Analiese's anatomy."

Mom's brow furrowed. "Okay?"

"Are you aware your daughter had a vestigial rib?" Dr. McGill asked, his froggy gaze levelled on mom.

Mom twitched. Like a spider. I stared at her, my heart staggering in my chest. All colour drained from her face.

"No." Her voice sounded strange and small, and

immediately, I knew something was off. Was mom lying? What on earth would make her lie about something as serious as this?

Dr. McGill continued. "We've seen vestigial ribs before, but the peculiar thing about Analiese's case is the rib is at the bottom of the thoracic cage. Highly irregular."

"What does that mean?" Mom asked. Oddly, she no longer looked sad or scared, now she looked irritated. Hostile.

"What it means is... your daughter's genetic makeup is unlike any other we've seen before," Dr. McGill said.

Another scientist, the one named Dr. Bomer, nodded in agreement. "Her existence will be of much interest to modern genetics around the world. Our studies of her genetic profile will be invaluable to our understanding of chromosomal abnormalities and to modern medicine."

Mom blinked, over and over, as if she was trying to blink away what she was hearing and seeing. "I don't understand."

"This situation is highly irregular. The opportunity for learning from your daughter's particular genetic makeup is endless. We believe it is possible her genetics may completely alter our current understanding of the human genome." Dr. Bomer smiled, an expression so out of place in the face of my mother's pain, it was almost unbearable to watch. He continued, "Everything we knew, or thought we knew is about to be challenged, all because of your daughter." The other doctors assembled around the table nodded in agreement.

"I don't know what to say." My mother's voice was quiet, like she was performing a stage whisper.

"We'll need to keep Analiese's body here for a period of time so we can administer all of the appropriate tests. We'll document our findings, as I'm sure you can appreciate." Dr. McGill gave mom a perfunctory smile and then addressed me directly. "But I'm also aware that you, Adriana, also have the atypical blood type."

"That's correct." The words that came out of my mouth were stiff, bordering on defensive. But I had nothing to be defensive about, did I? My muscles were stiff as petrified wood.

"Are Analiese and Adriana your biological children, Carla?" McGill asked.

"Yes, they are."

"We would like to contact the biological father," Dr. McGill said.

Mom glanced at me, her eyes wide. "I can supply you with that information. Why do you need it?"

Dr. McGill glanced at the other scientists. "Homozygous, or recessive traits, are typically inherited when both parents are carriers of the traits. Their father and you would both be carriers of recessive traits."

I thought about dad, and how his colouring, his body shape and his facial structure—blonde, brown-eyed, and six-foot-two was nothing like me, mom and Analiese. I realized there was a heavy silence hanging over the room. Mom's complete lack of response was very curious to say the least. I examined her widened eyes, the whites flashing. She only ever looked like this when she was truly afraid. The first time I'd ever seen her look like this was when she and Dad had a fight that resulted in him leaving. The first of many times he left us. Until he finally left for good.

"We would like to invite you, Adriana, and your mother and father to stay here at our lab so we can run some simultaneous tests on you and your sister. It's not that often we have the opportunity to cross-analyze genetically identical twins." Dr. Halan smiled widely.

"Oh?" I said. I glanced at mom whose eyes were completely round now, like saucers.

"Our studies on you, Carla, and Adriana's father would be relatively short, and could be conducted at a distance, in your home city, if necessary, but," Dr. McGill, his expression placid, continued, "Adriana, we'd like you to stay a bit longer. In the field of genetics, it is not uncommon to find genetic anomalies in the human population. But it is rare for the anomaly to be in identical twins. We are requesting you consider participating in some standard testing. For the purpose of scientific advancement, of course."

"How long would that take?" I asked.

"Good question." Dr. McGill glanced around the room and down at Analiese's file. "Perhaps one week, maximum, two."

"I'm in college. I don't know if I can afford to miss two weeks of classes. Besides, where would I stay?" I asked.

"I'm certain the University would be a willing participant in this research effort. We've made arrangements like this before. We will request your assignments, class notes and assigned readings during your stay with us. We can even moderate any quizzes or exams, if necessary." McGill's eyes looked bright, as if he took my question as a sign that I was softening to the idea. "And we have all of our participants stay at an adjacent residence, attached to the main building. The accommodations are luxurious, and," he smiled, "The food is excellent."

"The Endosymbiotic Theory could be tested as well," Dr. Bomer added, his words digressive at the end of his statement, as if he realized he'd said something out of turn.

Dr. McGill shot him a look, a gaze that held some sort of meaning. He turned back to me. "What do you think?"

"Okay, I suppose I could stay," I started.

Suddenly Mom stood up, her abrupt movement catching all eyes at the table. "Absolutely not. You've already interfered with my family too much. Bringing Analiese's body here and doing tests on her without even consulting me or her father is completely unacceptable. It's an invasion of privacy and a breach of her constitutional rights as a citizen, not to mention unprofessional conduct toward me and her father. And now you expect my only remaining daughter to become your guinea pig, after how we've been treated?"

"Mom." I stared at her. What happened to her manners? Clearly they all disappeared the day Analiese died. "I think what they're asking is reasonable."

"No. This is unacceptable." Mom shook her head. Back and forth, back and forth. Her heavily hair sprayed bob hardly moved.

Dr. McGill remained seated and leaned back in his chair. His colleagues sat motionless, some expressionless, others frowning. "Carla, our institute has acted in accordance with the laws of our country and the ethics of all governing bodies."

"You can call me Ms. Sinclair." Mom's skin was blotchy and red, her eyes wild. "I don't care. This is my daughter we're talking about."

"Mom. I think you're overreacting here—"

She turned to me, and the way she looked stopped the words from exiting my mouth. Her aqua eyes were glassy and red-rimmed, her lips quivering. "Come on. We're leaving before they decide they can keep you here against your will."

Dr. Bomer stood up. "Mrs. Sinclair. Please consider the wonderful contribution our research could make to medical science. Your daughter may lead us to important medical and genetic breakthroughs. We are not asking she stay here indefinitely. We simply would like her to stay a few weeks."

I startled when mom grabbed my arm with an iron fist. Like in the haze of a strange, vivid dream I followed her out of the room, only having enough time to cast a passing glance back at the scientists sitting around the table.

"Mom," I said under my breath.

Every one of the scientists had the same furrowed-brow look, including Dr. McGill.

"Hush," Mom commanded. Her voice had a familiar tone from my childhood, a tone with a wordless message, *don't say another damn word.*

"You are taking this out of context, Ms. Sinclair. We are only interested in what we can learn from your daughter's passing." McGill said as we exited the room. "Adriana, if you change your mind, you know where we are. I beg you to consider our request."

"I will," I said, my mother dragging me along. "Sorry about this."

We left the building, my mother tugging my arm the entire way. She pulled me along the corridor, into the elevator, and through the foyer. Once we were outside the heavy glass doors, I spoke. "What the hell was that about?" I demanded.

She glanced around, as if scanning for a hidden camera. Was she going crazy? Having some kind of paranoid delusion after Analiese's death? I'd heard of intense stress causing psychotic episodes in people, but I'd never seen any sign of mental illness in Mom before.

"We're not talking about this. Not now. Not here," Mom said.

"Why not?" I asked. "Please don't go all crazy paranoid on me."

Mom snapped back. "I told you I'm not talking about it here! Do you understand?"

I'd never in my life seen her look so unhinged. We returned to the hotel, her avoiding eye contact, me peppering her with questions she refused to answer, my volume growing with each rebuke. All I got was a variation of the same vague response: *I wasn't comfortable with what they were asking of you.* I seethed in response to her silence, with little effect. In bed, I tossed and turned and my mind raced as I listened to my mother's heavy snore beside me. *Fuck.*

The next morning, on our flight home, mom was twitchy and jumpy, like a deer in hunting season. Big brother over her shoulder. *Maybe the government is tuned into our radio channel, mom, to pick up our brainwaves.* All she was missing was the tin foil hat. I continued to ask questions with increased frustration, her continually evading me, until she finally muttered between gritted teeth, *Don't ask me until we are at home.*

I sat throughout the flight with my eyes closed, my outer body the perfect image of calm, hiding the turbulence inside of me.

#

It wasn't until we were safely inside her house that Mom looked like she actually inhaled a full breath.

"You can't put me off any longer. Jesus, there's no one

here, listening to us or taping our conversation, all right?" Jet-lagged and emotionally disturbed by her behavior, I had more than lost my patience.

Her eyes widened and her nostrils flared. "I'm not putting you off."

"Absolutely, you are. Answer my question. Do you have an extra rib, mom?"

"No."

"Have you had your blood typed? Do you have the same blood type Analiese and I have?"

Mom's expression darkened. "No, I don't. I'm O-negative."

"Why do I feel like there's something you're not saying? Or something you're afraid to say?" I stepped toward her and she shuffled backward like I had a contagious disease.

She sat down on a kitchen chair. Her mouth clamped shut and her eyes narrowed. "Adriana, this is serious. I don't think you realize just how serious this is."

"So serious you think NHGRI is going to use me like a lab rat?" I said. "So serious that you think people are lurking around every corner, listening to us, bugging our phone? Come on. You're losing it."

"Stop it, Adriana."

I threw my hands in the air and cursed. "I'm just trying to figure out what the hell is going on. Why can't you tell me what you know?"

Mom shook her head and ran her hands through her hair. "They took Analiese's body without our permission, which is bad enough, but when they said it was all done legally, that's when I realized you could be forced to stay at the lab, even if you don't want to."

"I gathered you think that from what you said to them." I paused. "But Mom, if they insisted, I would go, because obviously, it would be for an important reason."

Mom let out an odd chuckle. "Important to them, sure. Make you into a guinea pig to run tests and experiments so they can get their kicks. Meanwhile, your quality of life disappears."

"That's a little conspiratorial, isn't it?" I tried to hide the sick feeling I felt inside. Her mental health status was clearly far worse than I'd estimated. "Besides, they said two weeks. That's hardly going to affect my quality of life."

Mom's eyes widened. "You think I'm exaggerating? I know what loopholes the government has so they can get around the constitution. I know they can take you against your will if they want, they can suspend your rights if they deem it necessary and imprison you in a lab until they're damn good and satisfied."

My head throbbed and my hands fisted. "Okay...?"

Mom's lips pursed as she examined my face. "As a child, I remember rumblings in the family, things said in hushed tones between family members. They thought I was out of earshot, but I heard. Something about someone's blood. Our family has secrets."

Silence filled the air between us, heavy and still. Secrets? Finally, she was talking.

"Can you find out?" Tears stung at the back of my eyes at the possibility. If those secrets had been out in the open, could Analiese's death been prevented?

She nodded. "I'll try. In the meantime, can you please just... go back to college, go to class, blend in, pretend everything is normal, okay? Give me two days, and I'll dig around. I'll find us some answers."

*Mutation:*
*A relatively permanent change in hereditary material involving*
*either a physical change in chromosome relations or a*
*biochemical change in the codons that make up genes.*
*-Merriam-Webster Dictionary*

## CHAPTER THREE

### KALAN KANE

I sat across the aisle from the gorgeous girl, looking out of the corner of my eye, furtive glances, trying not to be noticed. There was something about her that was hard to put into words, an energy that practically pulsed off of her. She hadn't even said a word, and yet I couldn't keep myself from staring. I felt like a dog, watching my master's every move, waiting for some small gesture. Some small acknowledgement of my existence. I forced myself to turn in my seat so I wouldn't be tempted to stare at her. I didn't need to send her the creep vibe before I'd even met her. And meeting her was the ultimate goal.

Sitting through a Biochemistry lab wasn't something I was overly excited about, but I knew it was the only way I'd be able to see her up close. In fact, Stonewood, the small, relatively isolated university town right in the middle of a densely forested area, was one of the last places on my list of locations to visit. But here I was, all because of this girl, whose sister's death was in the paper, the headline reading, *'Patient with atypical blood type dies from botched blood transfusion.'*

She leaned down from her lab stool and rummaged through her backpack until she located the object she was in search of. She withdrew her hand from the pack to reveal a shiny red apple. Without hesitation, her lush lips pulled back and she bit down on the crimson skin, her incisors slicing through to the juicy flesh beneath. The familiar crunch echoed through the lab followed by the crisp, sweet scent that took me back to my childhood lunchroom.

I evaluated her features. She had at least one of the classic markers I was hoping she had. In fact, those teal green eyes of hers could be noticed halfway across the room. Even though she already had her lab coat on, it was obvious she also had a great rack, more than a handful, for sure. *Get your mind out of the gutter.*

The girl continued to chomp her fruit as she prepared her lab table. She adjusted her Bunsen burner so it sat directly in front of her, set her safety goggles to her right, and the evaporating dish and an Erlenmeyer flask to her left.

Judging by the numerous guys twisting at their desks, I wasn't the only one looking at her, either. A guy around her age sat in the next aisle over, not even trying to hide his kicked-puppy stare. She glanced over at him and he said "hi". Then I heard her voice for the first time.

"Derek." Her voice sounded as if her throat was pinched. Was there history between these two? Or was her voice like this on account that she had just lost her sister?

Derek's hound-dog expression transformed. "Hi. Look, we need to talk."

Her silky black hair swayed across her back as she spoke. A funny sound came from her mouth, like a stifled sob. "No, Derek, we don't. There is nothing we need to say to each other."

"I don't agree," Derek said. His expression was stricken. "I heard you went to Maryland. Why were you there?"

Adriana's eyes grew wet and the colour went from teal to a deep turquoise. "They took Analiese's body to the National Human Genome Research Institute," Adriana said in a tight voice. She no longer held back her tears and one zigzagged down her cheek in an inky streak.

My heart rate spiked. Obviously this was the girl. And the news article I'd read about the atypical blood was, in fact, her sister, and if her sister had some genetic quirks... perhaps Adriana did, too?

Derek's eyebrows crinkled in the middle. "Why?"

Adriana's expression changed, grew... uneasy. She surveyed the entire room, and then did a double take. What was she looking for?

"We have a weird blood type."

*Bingo.*

"Geez, I wish I could have been there for you." Derek said, his expression sympathetic in a greasy way. "I'm sorry. I'm so... sorry."

Adriana's head tilted forward so her hair cascaded over the top of her desk like hundreds of long black ribbons. She shook her head. "Don't."

I wished I could have seen her face at that moment.

Derek's expression returned immediately to that of undisguised pain, his mouth pursed into a tight, flat line. He put his head down on his arms atop his desk. Adriana turned in her seat, her back to him, her expression dark, her arms folded across her chest.

Then a couple walked in, chatting loudly, both smiling at Adriana. The woman was petite with highlighted hair and dark skin, her exotic bone structure and almond eyes making me immediately think she was from the Philippines. She took a seat in front of me, and the guy, a blond with orange pants and orange shirt, sat down across the aisle so he was sitting in front of Adriana.

"Hi," Adriana said, her mouth barely pulled up at the corners into a half-smile. I could imagine myself sucking on those lips and the thought of it made my belly clench. She took another bite of apple with perfect white teeth. She was gorgeous.

Derek nodded perfunctorily at them. "Tait. Zoe."

The guy, Tait, slapped Adriana's lab table. "A-dog," he said in a mock-ghetto voice. "We have great news." His smile exposed both upper and lower teeth. He had a Disney look to him, all perfectly styled, spikey blond hair and big, round eyes.

Zoe leaned across the aisle and set something in front of her. "Tonight. Seven tickets to the Ruminate concert. I decided we need to just forget about life for a few hours. A concert would be the perfect thing to take a break from… everything. It is okay to take breaks from grieving, you know. Are you in?"

Adriana stared at the concert tickets on the table in front of her. Derek gawked at the tickets as well, his mouth slightly open until he noticed me watching him. Then his eyes narrowed and he turned back toward the front of the class.

"How did you get them? I heard they were sold out." Adriana looked at the tickets as if they were worth a fortune.

"I was logged in and ready to click the moment the tickets went on sale," Tait said.

"Um, thanks, guys. But I can't. Not tonight. Sorry" Adriana smiled and handed them back to Zoe, who stuffed them into her purse. Then something stormy and tempestuous replaced Adriana's sunny expression.

The BioChem Professor strode in. He stood about six feet tall, with dark hair and horn-rimmed glasses. He quickly nodded to the class before he turned around and wrote his name on the blackboard. Dr. Johansen. Clearly, he wasn't interested in formal wear, opting for jeans and a t-shirt beneath his white lab coat. The cool professor. The, *I'm-cool-and-scholarly* type. I could just see him on his recumbent bike, his backpack for a briefcase in the carrying basket in front, pedalling home from his tough day teaching students about stuff they never thought about again after they wrote the final exam.

He turned back toward the class, and after awkwardly muttering his name and the title of the class, handed out the course syllabus. Then he launched into a lecture about mitochondrion outer and inner membranes composed of phospholipid bilayers and proteins. *What the hell have I gotten myself into?*

Adriana leaned back in her desk and dug into her pack again where her telephone buzzed. She was looking down at it when Dr. Johansen stopped speaking and glared at her.

"Excuse me," Dr. Johansen said, his eyes narrowing into slits. "You may not care about wasting your tuition dollars, but the other students here do."

A professor with a self-righteous streak and a hot temper. Great.

Adriana glanced up and a pink flush crept across her cheeks. She stuffed her phone back into her purse and nodded. "Sorry. I was listening."

"If you were listening, you would know the five distinct parts to a mitochondrion. Can you recite them for the class, please?" Dr. Johansen asked. His face twisted up into a mocking smile. Self-righteous and condescending. Charming.

Adriana looked down. "Oh, um... okay. The outer mitochondrial membrane, the intermembrane space, the inner mitochondrial membrane, and.... I'm sorry. I can't remember."

"The cristae space and the matrix," I said, levelling my gaze on Dr. Johansen. The professor's eyes glazed over. Out of the corner of my eye, I could see that Adriana was looking right at me. She smiled and mouthed, *Thank you*. I smiled back, lost in this moment, our gazes locked. Until Dr. Johansen cleared his throat.

I looked up at him and noticed how his expression was somewhat more relaxed. "I don't think I asked you, Mr...?"

"Kane, sir," I said. "My name is Kalan Kane."

"Well, Mr. Kane. I didn't ask you for the answer, did I?" Self-importance oozed from the man, but in a schoolyard bully way. I didn't like him. Not one bit.

"Sorry, Doctor," I said with complete neutrality.

The prof's face softened even further, and a tiny, self-impressed smile tugged the sides of his mouth up. "Fine. Don't do it again." He turned back to the board and began to write out the words I'd recited.

Adriana half-turned in her seat, her lips tucked together to stifle a smile. Was it possible she was what I hoped she was? Her evocative eyes were the exact hue of the identifying gene marker. Her waist was tiny, and she had a long torso as well, a probable sign of the other marker. And the sister stuff... It probably wasn't really a question of whether she was one. The question was, did she even know what she was?

Class ended and the students filed toward the door. I took my time cleaning up and putting lab supplies away, placing my books into my backpack with slow precision, to kill time. Out of the corner of my eye, I saw Adriana nod to her friends before they left. When my books were all securely in place, I straightened up. She was looking right at me.

"Hi," Adriana said as she gathered her backpack and swung it over her shoulder. She stepped forward and as she drew nearer, an infusion of her scent filled the air, a lovely combination of soap and raspberries. The mixture made my head spin and my mouth water. "I'm Adriana," she said.

"Hi, I'm Kalan."

"I wanted to thank you for stepping up like that. It's not often someone will take on Johansen. He's got quite the reputation for being a hot-head. Last year a student from a course on social deviance was hanging around in his classroom, acting like a... well, a social deviant, and Johansen lost it. His face turned all purple and he started screaming and freaking out." Adriana rolled her eyes. "Anyway, thanks. I'm heading to my next class. You?"

"You're welcome. And yes, I'm heading to my next class too." I followed her out the door and we set off down the bleach-scented hallway, the janitor halfway down the hall, mopping away. "Which room are you in?"

I was interrupted by a jeering call that originated from a group of mammoth-sized guys lingering against a windowsill. "Wow, that is quite a tan, dude." A few of them were grinning while others looked away, as if pretending nothing happened. I was used to these kinds of comments. I'd been called worse.

Adriana shot them a glare. "So rude," she said, loud enough for them to hear. We continued to walk. "Sorry about that."

"That's nothing compared to what I've been called before," I said.

"I hope you don't mind me asking, but are you... albino? Sorry, is that even a politically correct term?"

We took a few more steps down the hall before I finally answered. "Yeah. I have Acromia. It's a genetic anomaly."

"Right. Albinism affects approximately one in twenty thousand people," Adriana said, looking up at me through a thick fringe of black lashes. "Remembered it from first-year Bio."

"Impressive. And do you remember why?" I smiled. "Why I have white hair, the white skin?"

Adriana's eyes widened. "The absence of an enzyme involving the production of melanin," she said as if describing the ingredients involved in making Kraft Dinner. "Have you ever had the genetic test?"

"Yes. But it only served to confirm what I already knew."

We approached a corner, where it was clear we were about to part ways. "I'm heading this way," Adriana said, examining my face so closely my nerves began to sing. "Hey—what about your eyes? They aren't pink," Adriana's own pupils dilated, endlessly black within a tiny ring of pale teal.

I nodded, swallowing against a lump in my throat. "I know. They're more—"

"Silver," Adriana interrupted in a liquid voice. She stepped forward and set warm fingers on my jaw, tilting my face down for a closer look. I swallowed. She was far more... assertive than what I'd expected. Her finger pressure was tight, but the skin of her hand was warm, soft. Her scent curled up around me once again, the heady infusion so sweet and so potent I got light-headed.

Her eyes shimmered, her mouth slightly open. Few girls had ever been this close to me before, especially a girl who also happened to look like a model. My cheeks warmed.

"Silver eyes. So cool," Adriana said. She let go of my jaw.

It was obvious we were about to part ways. *Shit.*

"What is your next class?" Adriana asked.

"Actually," I said, "I'm thinking of ditching my next class and heading over to Starbucks for coffee. I just can't settle into the whole routine yet."

Adriana checked her watch. "You know, I can't settle in yet either. Could I join you?"

"Sure." My voice almost cracked. The last thing I needed was to sound like a prepubescent boy in front of her.

The Starbucks was across the street from campus, and we

were in line waiting for our coffee within twenty minutes. We sat down at a booth, side by side, which was too bad because I really liked looking right at her. Oh, well. I was just happy she wanted to be here. With me.

"Kalan, tell me about yourself. What are you passionate about?"

I chuckled. She was very forward, but in a sweet, compelling way. "I like to fish, watch action movies and take long walks in the park."

Adriana gave me a poke with her elbow. "Good one. But this isn't The Dating Game. Seriously."

I shrugged. Who was I? What did I tell her? I'm an orphan, a throwaway child whose mother thought it best if I went into foster care and whose foster parents never felt the need to legally adopt me? That I'd grown up my entire life thinking I was a waste of skin, a freak of nature, an outsider? That I'd never know love? No, I couldn't tell her those things. Not if I wanted to ever see her again.

"I don't know," I said, "I guess I'm still trying to figure that out. As for passion, I'm not sure I've found one yet."

Adriana nodded and took a long sip of her coffee, surveying me over the top of her frothy mug. "Me, either. There's just so much pressure at our age to make decisions, decisions that will affect the rest of our lives. This year I have to pick a major. But what if I pick the wrong one? What if I decide to go into economics and then realize I can't handle sitting at a desk all day? Or what if I go into teaching and realize I really hate working with children? It's too much pressure."

My coffee scalded the tip of my tongue and I lowered my cup back to the table. "I agree. I wish there was some way of predicting the future. Some way to see the outcome of all our decisions. A fast-forward."

Adriana let out a long breath. "I'm happy to find someone who agrees with me. It's so annoying to be around people who know exactly what they want to do, and the exact steps they need to take to get it. That's what my friends are like, Zoe and Tait."

"It would be easier," I said. "What do they want to do?"

"Tait's major is computer science. Zoe is going to apply to be a teacher."

"They're lucky. The hard part is over for them. The decision part, anyway." I paused. "I also wish there was some way to see what our overall lives would be like in the future. Like, who do we marry? Do we have kids? Do we stay together or get divorced? That way, you could save yourself so much wasted time, dating people you aren't going to be with."

"Like a map of life," Adriana said, her eyes mischievous. "Take the fork in the road to the right, you'll get married but eventually divorced. Take the left, stay single but happy."

"A roadmap to life." I chuckled.

Adriana cast a sidelong look at me. "It sounds like you're

in quite a hurry to find the right person. The one you're going to stay married to forever."

Shit. I'd clearly revealed far too much. "Doesn't everybody?"

Her forehead wrinkled. "Hell, no. Most guys are only interested—"

I cut her off. "In one thing, right?"

"It's true." One of her eyebrows rose. "Maybe not every guy. But most guys."

"Well, I guess I'm not most guys."

She turned to look at me face to face. Her turquoise eyes were so bright in the windows it was like looking into a Christmas light. "Fair enough. Maybe you're not most guys."

I shrugged. "Let's get back to our roadmap to life concept. I say we create an app and get rich off of it? We could call it LifeMap."

'The LifeMapApp!" Adriana let out a long laugh. "You're a funny guy."

Her high-pitched giggle sounded girlish and sweet, totally contagious. After several minutes of this, and having attracted the stares of all the patrons and baristas, we finally quieted down.

"And you are a funny girl."

Adriana smiled, and then that smile fell and was replaced by a clouded expression. She climbed out of her seat and swung her backpack over her shoulder. "I need to get going, Kalan. Will I see you in class tomorrow?"

"Definitely," I said.

She walked out of the coffee shop and I watched as she returned to campus, her footfalls so swift she was nearly running. I looked at my watch. Her class wasn't even over yet. Where was she off hurrying to?

#

The next day in class, Adriana looked completely different. She had red-rimmed eyes and barely any makeup on. Her hair was pulled back in a ponytail and she had her fall coat on, the collar straight up so it covered the lower half of her pink, blotchy face.

There was no doubt she'd been crying.

After class was over, she ducked out so fast I almost didn't see it. I hustled down the hall to catch up to her.

"Hey," I said, falling into step beside her. A very fast clip. "Is everything okay?"

Adriana didn't respond, her chin tucked down into her black jacket. Her arms were crossed tight across her chest. She cast a furtive glance my way and then back.

"What's wrong?"

A funny sound emerged from where her mouth was buried beneath the collar of her coat. "Nothing. I'm fine."

I kept up with her, the speed of her pace ever increasing. We were damn near in a full-out jog. "Wait. Something's wrong. Is there something I can do?"

She stopped abruptly. So abruptly that it took me a few steps to slow my momentum. I turned around to see her heading in the other direction.

"I'm not trying to bug you here. I'm just concerned. Obviously you're not fine."

She stopped again and turned to face me. "Is there a reason you can't take a hint? Is there something preventing you from fucking off?"

I took a step back. Then I reminded myself, if this was the twin sister of the girl in the paper, then she was obviously very emotional. I held up my hands in an 'I give' gesture. "Look. I'm just worried. I wanted to make sure you're alright. But if you want me to fuck off, then I'll leave you alone."

Her shoulders slumped and she stuck even more of her head into her collared jacket. "No. I'm not alright." Her voice was muffled through the fabric.

I stepped toward her, careful not to get too close. "Do you want to talk about it?"

Like a turtle, her head came out, just a bit, enough for me to see streaks of tears on her cheeks. She wiped them off on the back of her palm and then thrust her hands into her pockets.

"My sister was in a car accident a week ago." Immediately, Adriana's eyes re-filled. The tears turned her eyes an almost preternatural shade of turquoise, the colour of a tropical ocean.

My gut tightened. "I'm sorry."

Adriana shook her head. "She died." Two fat teardrops spilled from Adriana's eyes.

I stepped closer, considered putting a hand on her shoulder but clasped them together instead. "Nobody should have to lose their loved one that way."

She looked down, her eyes re-filling with moisture. "I feel so stupid to be telling you this at school. Now I'll be bawling my head off all day."

"I know this probably won't help, but..." I watched a huge tear pool at the bottom of her eye, and when it tipped out, I swept it from her cheek. Idiot. Way too intimate. "I've heard time heals."

Adriana's tears came in currents now. She lowered her head.

All of a sudden, my thumb grew warm and turned into an odd burning sensation. It reminded me of a wound doused in rubbing alcohol. I looked at it. The skin was growing redder by the second.

"I'll be right back." I walked away, despite the surprised look on her face.

*"I lead the Human Genome Project, which has now revealed all of the 3 billion letters of our own DNA instruction book. I am also a Christian. For me, scientific discovery is also an occasion of worship."*
*- Francis Collins Director, National Human Genome Research Institute*

## CHAPTER FOUR

### ADRIANA SINCLAIR

Kalan returned from the bathroom just as my cell phone rang in my pocket. "Just a sec," I said, pulling the phone from my jeans. I checked the caller ID. Mom. Undoubtedly checking to see if I'd made it through another class without leaving halfway through or having a nervous breakdown. I had. I guess I'd passed a hurdle. Sort of. Maybe I shouldn't have. "Hi, Mom. Have you found anything?"

Kalan watched me with inscrutable eyes as my mother's voice exploded in my ear. "Nothing yet. I'm going to visit grandma today. Have you told NHGRI you're not interested? Because if you don't, they'll just keep hounding you."

I took a deep breath. "I'm going to go to NGHRI, Mom."

Silence on the other end stretched out, and I wondered if she'd hung up or dropped the phone. I jumped when she finally spoke again. "No," her voice was a breathy whisper. I knew from years of interactions with my mother that she was fighting back tears, and if they came out, I probably wouldn't be able to stand up to them. Her tears could crumble my resolve like rain washing away sand. I had to get off the phone. Fast.

"Mom, they're asking for my voluntary cooperation. There's nothing conspiratorial going on. I'm a scientific anomaly, that's all." I heard gasping through the phone. "Look, I'm talking to someone right now, I'll call you later and we can discuss it then, okay?" She responded with a choked garble. The floodgates were nearly open. Less than thirty seconds left. "Tonight. At six. See you then." I hung up, turned my cell off and shoved it into my backpack. Then I looked up at Kalan. "My mom. She's still raw. We both are."

"Of course you would be," he said.

I gulped in a breath. "I'm going away for a few weeks. Out of state. I'll be leaving as soon as I talk to all of my Profs. I need to go talk to Dr. Johansen so I can get my assignments and make arrangements. I'm heading to his office right now. Do you want to walk with me? I don't think he's teaching right now."

"Sure," Kalan said.

The academic offices were just an elevator ride away. We got in, and I pushed the button for the fourth floor. The elevator motor whirred as we went up.

"You mentioned you are going out of state. Where to?"

Kalan asked.

The elevator slowed and the doors opened to the fourth floor. We got out and walked toward Dr. Johansen's office.

"To the National Human Genome Research Institute for genetic testing," I said. "You're probably wondering why. It's a long story."

Kalan had an odd look on his face, and I could tell he wanted to ask me something, but we'd arrived at Dr. Johansen's office. I knocked on the partly open door.

"Come in," said Professor Grumpy.

Kalan waited outside as I entered the office. It was small inside, barely bigger than a bedroom. The gigantic oak desk situated in the middle took up the majority of floor space. It smelled funny in here, sour, like formaldehyde mixed with something tinny. He had piles of papers strewn about on one side of his desk, coil-ringed booklets stacked one on top of the other on the other side of his desk, texts in the middle, several of them so far off the edge it was a mere bump away from a textbook avalanche.

Dr. Johansen was writing furiously on a document in red ink. He didn't get up when we walked in. "Come in. I'll be with you in a moment."

I stood there, awkwardly waiting as he ignored me. I glanced around. Several framed degrees hung behind him as well as four strategically placed art canvases of abstract images. One canvas was red and black, one purple and pink, one green and yellow, and one white and black. They were all similar in theme, twisting vines vaguely in the shape of a double helix. Or maybe polypeptide chains, I wasn't sure. The canvas in black and white had one red apple at the bottom left, near the edge.

"Dr. Johansen, I'm Adriana Sinclair, I'm in your Bio Chemistry two-thirteen class. I was wondering if—"

Johansen cut me off. "You need some sort of special consideration?"

"Yes." I swallowed.

"What can I do for you?"

I launched into the story of Analiese's death. *Twinkilled.* "I've been asked to participate in some testing at the National Human Genome Research Institute in Maryland."

Johansen's eyebrows went up and his eyes brightened. "I see."

I continued, "They're suggesting it will take a couple of weeks. I was hoping I could get the assigned readings and assignments so I could continue in your class while I'm at the Institute?"

"Okay," Dr. Johansen said, staring at me, his eyes unblinking. Then he seemed to focus. "You'll be missing a number of labs in two weeks and it's hard to do lab learning by distance. I suppose I could meet with you privately upon your return to help you catch up…"

"I've been assured by the geneticists at NHGI that every attempt will be made to help me continue my schooling."

"I'll see what I can do. But there is only so much I am able to do to help. Part of your success will be dependent on you," Dr. Johansen said. "If you successfully pass the standardized exams, there isn't problem. However, if you don't, you may want to consider dropping the course before the mark becomes part of your permanent record."

"Okay."

"This is an exceptional situation," Dr. Johansen said. "I'm sorry it is under such awful circumstances."

I nodded. He stared at me again for far too long before he began gathering up papers from various file folders on and in his desk.

He handed me several sets of stapled pages. "Here are the lab instructions for the labs you'll be missing over the next two weeks," he paused and held out another set of papers, "And these are the assigned readings."

"Do we have any tests?" I asked.

"No," he said.

I put the papers in my backpack and zipped it up, ready to go.

"Did they mention what tests they intend to do?" he asked.

"No," I said. Then I thought about the off-the-cuff remark Dr. Bomer made while we were at the institute. The one Dr.

McGill seemed unimpressed by. "But the one geneticist mentioned something I haven't looked up yet. Have you heard of the Endosymbiotic theory?"

His eyes narrowed. "Yes, of course. I'm surprised you haven't learned of it yet, being that you're in second year," I held his gaze. Finally, he continued, "The thrust of the theory is based on the idea that mitochondria originated as symbioses between two independent, free-living, single-celled organisms that were taken inside another cell as an endosymbiont."

"So, mitochondria is the product of symbiosis?" I asked. "As in, the mitochondrial DNA of humans was once a parasitic organism?"

"That's the theory in a nutshell, yes. I want to show you something." Dr. Johansen grasped a textbook off of his bookshelf, one titled *Illustrated Biochemistry*. I peered at the cover of the book. His name was listed as one of the contributing authors. He flipped it open to a specific page and held it up so I could see, like a kindergarten teacher during story time. It was an image portraying the evolution of the theory. "This illustration is of a host cell and ingested bacteria. It shows how it's possible that, over time, they could become dependent on one another for survival. Over time, this dependence could result in a permanent relationship. Millions of years of evolution later, those mitochondria and chloroplasts would become highly specialized to the point where today they can no longer survive outside the cell."

I stared at the image at the right corner of the text, the image of a fat blue host cell and two, bean-shaped bacterium. I didn't truly understand the meaning of what he'd said, other than the basic biological concepts I'd learned last year in Bio.

"Do you understand?" Dr. Johansen asked.

"Sort of," I said. "But what does this theory have to do with me and Analiese?"

Dr. Johansen smiled, his teeth stained greyish yellow. He looked better with his mouth closed. "Perhaps you are about to find out."

I nodded. The thought of being alone in Maryland, without Analiese, working through this homework and doing the labs on my own suddenly made me feel weary. Dropping the course seemed like a highly desirable option. "Thank you. I'll be in touch."

"Feel free to contact me when you return. I'd like to hear about your experience at the Institute," Dr. Johansen said.

I left his office and found Kalan still waiting for me, right outside the door, texting. "Hi," he said. We started off down the hall. "It sounds like he's going to try to help you."

"Yeah," I glanced back. We were well out of Dr. Johansen's earshot now. "Sort of. He basically said if I fail the tests, it's my problem. No special arrangements, I guess. Not even for the NHGRI."

"I've been there," Kalan said, "To the NHGRI. Both me

and my brother, Marcus. My twin."

The word *twin* caused a zap of sensation in my ribcage. Like my heart was hit by lightning. "You have a twin, too?" This was either very coincidental or very, very creepy. I wasn't sure which.

"Yes, but we didn't grow up together," Kalan said. "In fact, we didn't meet until we were both fifteen."

Why would twins be separated? I couldn't imagine a worse fate, having been separated from Analiese all those years. It would have been like having a phantom limb. I suddenly felt gratitude for the years I'd had with my sister, as rocky as they were. I blinked back tears.

Kalan explained before I had to ask the obvious. "Marcus and I were given up at birth."

"Oh," I said. "I'm sorry."

Kalan shrugged. "It is what it is."

"Who raised you?"

"Foster parents," Kalan said. "They're the only parents I've ever known. I'm lucky. They've been very good to me."

"And your brother? You said you didn't meet him until you were fifteen?"

"He had adoptive parents," Kalan paused and bit his lip. "Things weren't great for him."

"And now you are both here? In Stonewood?" I asked. "Why?"

"Marcus and I are looking for our birth mother. She was apparently here in Stonewood the last time she was seen."

"The last time she was seen?" I asked.

"From what I understand, she was sketchy." Kalan scratched his chin. His knuckles could be seen though his pale skin like it was transparent shrink wrap. "She's had a few pseudonyms over the years, first it was Janet Kaar, then Jennifer Robinson. When she lived in Stonewood, she was known as Jenna or Jeannie Wright. Have you ever heard of her?"

"No, sorry," I said. "Do you have any leads?"

Kalan shook his head and looked directly at me. "None. All I know are those names and the fact that her hair was black, she has blue-green eyes and... she has an extra rib."

I felt like I'd been punched in the stomach. "An extra rib?"

Kalan nodded, his gaze fixed on my face.

"I have an extra rib. And so did my sister."

A wave of emotion passed through Kalan's expression, an emotion I couldn't identify. "I knew it."

"You knew what?" I asked.

Kalan smiled. "Marcus and I were right. You have all of the genetic markers. The blood, the eyes, the rib. More pieces of the puzzle."

My breath caught in my throat, momentarily. "Do I have something to do with your mother?" I asked. "Are we related or something?"

Kalan shrugged. "I've been through the same blood analysis that you have," Kalan said. "That's why Marcus and I were at NHGRI."

I nearly tripped over my own feet. Instead, I came to a dead stop in the middle of the hallway of the Arts and Science building. Two sets of twins with an unknown blood type. What were the odds? "I have so many questions right now I don't know where to start. How did you end up at NHGRI?"

"Marcus's parents. I lived in foster care all these years, but Marcus was adopted. His adoptive parents were... different, but I'll tell you about them later. They wanted to stockpile his blood because they worried he might need it, in case he got sick or injured. Anyway, when they began the process, they learned his blood didn't quite fit into slot A or B."

"When did you find out?" I asked.

"Luckily nothing ever happened that required my needing to give or receive blood. I didn't find out until after I'd met Marcus,"

"How did you meet him?"

Kalan sucked in a breath. "His parents were... different, as I mentioned before. I think they saw Marcus like he was some kind of porcelain doll, one that they wanted to be handsome and perfect, but not have any needs. Most people would assume I was the one who would have had a difficult childhood, since I never left the foster system, but I was the fortunate one. Marcus's parents were really hard on him. If he'd been born in the Victorian era, it may have been common to have the *children will be seen and not heard* mentality, but not now. Marcus ended up angry, resentful and self-absorbed." Kalan turned to me. "I'm getting to your answer, just bear with me a moment." I nodded and Kalan continued. "His parents wanted to know every aspect to Marcus's development and heredity. Our mother apparently tried to keep the information about our being twins as hush-hush as she could, but hospitals have records and so do state departments. They found out about me and where I lived, and when Marcus was old enough, they arranged for him to meet me."

"God. That must have been amazing, to find out you weren't alone, that you had a biological twin?"

Kalan chuckled, a hapless sound. "You would think so, wouldn't you? But no. Unfortunately, Marcus and I were unable to... connect. He and I are very different. You'll see when you meet him."

"So, he's difficult?" I asked.

"That is a very accurate descriptor." Kalan chuckled again, this time a much happier sound.

"You and Marcus came to Stonewood after you heard Analiese died, in the hopes of finding me, didn't you?"

Kalan's smile fell. "Yes."

I wasn't sure what to think. Or feel. My skin tingled. "Where are you and Marcus from?"

"I'm from Livingston, Montana. Marcus is from Minneapolis." Kalan paused. "We read in the headlines that you were enrolled in college here, so we came. I found your name on the class list outside the Dean's office."

So much for anonymity and the protection of my confidential demographic information. "Oh."

"Look, I realize this is a lot to take in, and I'm sure your mind is absolutely overloaded after everything that's happened... Analiese dying, learning about the blood type, and about me and Marcus. But I promise you, we just want to understand why we're like this. And we need to find our mother to figure it out."

"Is Marcus albino too?"

He smiled and shot a mischievous sidelong glance my way. "Wait and see."

#

I met Kalan in the parking lot of the three story hotel he was staying at on the outskirts of the city. We parked side by side. I got out of my compact car as he got out of his sedan. As we approached the white stucco building, he pulled a key card from his jeans pocket and we went in through a side door. Inside, vacuums whirred away by the housecleaning staff hard at work, the scent of industrial cleaner intermingling with something minty and fresh, tickling at the back of my throat. It was a decent hotel, the gold and red carpet soft and spongy beneath my feet, the white stucco on the outside echoed on the interior walls. Every few feet was an ornate oil painting in jewel tones set above a table that held a large red vase of flowers.

Kalan slowed as we approach room four-twelve. "He's waiting for us." He opened the door and stepped in, holding the door open for me to follow.

I stepped into the room and stopped midstride. My legs felt like they'd turned to spaghetti beneath me. The face smiling at me from the chair at the other end of the hotel room was exactly the same as Kalan, except the colouring. Where Kalan was fair, Marcus was tanned. Where Kalan's hair was a silvery-blonde, Marcus had a shock of pitch-black hair. Where Kalan's eyes were greyish-pewter, Marcus's were as black as shiny obsidian.

He smiled at me, the same winning smile that Kalan had. He stood up. "Hello. You must be Adriana. My name is Marcus. Marcus White."

"Hi, Marcus," I said. "Nice to meet you."

Marcus dipped his head forward in a gentlemanly gesture. "Has my brother filled you in on our quest?"

"Yes, he has."

"I'm surprised to see you. I wasn't sure you would agree to come with Kalan, especially so soon after meeting him," Marcus said.

Kalan shot him a look. "There was a turn of events. Adriana is going to NHGRI for testing."

Marcus's eyebrows shot up. "What kind of testing?"

I nodded. "I don't know yet. They weren't very specific. And the waiver is fairly generic. It doesn't go into detail about procedures."

"Oh. That changes things, doesn't it?" Marcus said.

"Why does it change things?" I asked.

Marcus looked at Kalan, and then back at me. "I was hoping we could ask you and any of your contacts a few questions. Help us generate ideas about where to start. Now we're going to lose time," Marcus said to Kalan.

This first impression of Marcus was not off to a good beginning. I already didn't particularly like him.

"Marcus, we can't expect Adriana to jump at helping us find our mother right now. She has other things on her mind. Besides, we've never even met our mother. We've gone almost twenty years without her. I think we can wait a little longer." Marcus pursed his lips together in response, but Kalan continued. "I personally think this situation with Analiese and Adriana is directly related to us. I bet we'll find out about our mother in the process."

Marcus looked skyward, his eyes almost a roll, but not quite. He was really not winning any points with me. "It doesn't look like we have much choice, does it?"

"We'll stay, do some digging on our own," Kalan was trying to smooth out Marcus's prickly attitude. "And we'll check in with Adriana in a day or so."

Marcus shrugged and peered at me, his mouth a tight line. "We don't know anyone here. It's going to be a lot harder trying to navigate this city on our own. We were really hoping you'd have some ideas for us, Adriana."

*Presumptuous prick.* "Sorry."

"I'm being rude, aren't I?" Marcus asked. "I don't mean to sound so self-absorbed, it's just that we've waited so long, and to have finally come here, and found you... I was starting to get excited about finally meeting my mother."

*Considerably less prick-ish.* I can introduce you to my friends, Tait and Zoe," I said. "I'm sure they'd be willing to show you around and help out." I didn't bother offering my mother, I knew she'd be about as cooperative as a cat going into a bathtub full of water.

Marcus's expression brightened considerably. "Perfect, yes. When can we meet them?"

I dug my phone out of my purse and texted a joint message: *Can u show someone around Stnwood?* Both responded almost simultaneously. Tait's response was, *Ya, who is it?* and Zoe's was, *K, who?*

"They said they would. I'll bring them over tonight," I said. I wanted to get to Bethesda as soon as possible, get some answers of my own.

Marcus smiled. "Great."

#

Introductions were arranged for that night at Kalan and Marcus's hotel. We met in the courtyard out back, where a pretty white gazebo was lit up inside with tiny white lights, lending a fairy tale feel to the evening. It was dusk, the mountains shadowed black against the indigo backdrop of the night sky. The autumn air was cool and crisp, and there was a faint scent of rotting fruit in the air. Marcus and Kalan hadn't yet arrived, so I took the opportunity to give Zoe and Tait the full explanation about Kalan and Marcus and the blood mystery we had in common.

Tait was first to respond. "This seems suspicious. The guy may as well have told you he is stalking you."

"It's not stalking if you tell the person right away," I said. "It's not like he followed me around for days on end. He came and found me and told me."

"Aren't you a little nervous to go to Maryland alone?" Zoe asked.

"Not really, no."

Was I afraid? Did I even know what I was getting into here? I shivered and shrugged it off. "At this point, with Analiese dead and my entire reality falling apart, I'm not feeling particularly patient. I definitely don't want to babysit my mother, whose mental health is seriously deteriorating."

Tait cocked his head to the side and his lips pinched together. "We'll come with you. All you have to do is ask." He glanced at Zoe. "Well, I would come. You know I would do anything for you, girl." Tait's personality shone as bright as a sun. Just being around him made some of the darkness within me wither up and retreat.

"I know," I said. "But I don't know when I'll be back. I'm willing to stay until I find out what's going on, and if it means I have to drop out of college this term, I'll do it. This is not your problem."

"If you're sure…" Tait said.

Footsteps approached us, two sets. It was them. Twin yin and yang. "Hi." I said, as soon as they stepped onto the platform. They looked amazing together, their faces and bodies exactly the same, their coloring the polar opposite. Kalan looked like some kind of fallen angel, his silver hair glossy in the glow of the tiny white lights. He wore a thin cotton t-shirt and jeans that showed off an athletic build. Beside him, Marcus's black hair shone almost blue. His shirt glowed in fiery shades with the band name Whitesnake across the front. The two of them side by side almost didn't look real. Two perfect specimens, models made to demonstrate the epitome of the male of the species, at opposite ends of the color spectrum.

"Hello, Adriana," Marcus said. His gaze swept across to Zoe, then to Tait.

"Hey," Kalan said to the group.

I did a round of introductions and after a moment or two we sat down on the concrete ledges of the gazebo. It was cold and hard against my bottom and a chill ran through me. Colorado fall evenings were always cool. Kalan and Marcus sat side by side on one end of the gazebo and me, Tait and Zoe on the other side.

"When will you leave for Maryland?" Zoe asked.

"Tomorrow," I said.

"Marcus and I are hoping we'll find some leads in Stonewood, maybe someone who knows something about our mother," Kalan said. "We were wondering if you would be willing to help us? We thought you might have some ideas, since you're from here."

Tait responded, his gaze on Marcus for a lingering moment before he spoke to Kalan. "Of course. We'll do anything to help out. We just want Adriana to figure out what happened to Analiese. We all loved her very much." Tait's voice broke on the last words, and his eyes filled.

A gasp burst from my own mouth and tears erupted from my eyes, streaming down my face. Tait put his arm around me and pulled me close. Temple to temple, he whispered soothing words to me in hushed tones until I got a grip on my relentless crying. When I opened my eyes, Kalan and Marcus were no longer across from me. They were talking outside the gazebo.

"Do you think this is okay? Showing them around?" I asked.

"They seem normal," Tait said. "I don't mind. Do you, Zoe?"

"Marcus gives me the creeps. Actually they both do." Zoe paused. "Then again, it's not every day I see people that look like... like that."

Kalan and Marcus re-entered the gazebo.

Marcus came to us and got down on his haunches in front of me. "Adriana, I'm so sorry for your loss." I nodded in acknowledgement and he stood back up. "Tait and Zoe, what do you think of our request?" His gaze lingered on Tait.

Tait leaned forward, closer to Marcus. "Sure. We'll help you."

Marcus set his hand on Tait's shoulder. "Thank you."

My phone buzzed in my pocket. I dug it out. *Damn.* "Hi, Mom."

"Hi, dear." Her speech was clipped and rapid, once again. It was like she was running on rocket fuel. "We are going to visit Grandma and Aunt Bethany tomorrow. They might have some history for us, maybe give us a lead."

This was a crimp in the plan, but would be a better plan than heading off without making sure we'd covered every base here first.

"Okay," I said.

"I'll meet you at Grandma's." I hung up. Tait observed me with a steadfast gaze. "There's a delay in my travel plans."

*Old Earth Creationism: An interpretation of Genesis in which days are taken to be figurative lengths of time, and the time scales given by geologists are generally correct. However, the special creation of man precludes common descent.*
*-Talk Origins*

## CHAPTER FIVE

### ADRIANA SINCLAIR

Ten more minutes before I had to leave for our visit with Grandma and Aunt Bethany. I quickly opened up my laptop and typed in the keywords, *extra+rib+bloodline.* Search results came up, all of the websites conspiracy theorists who referred to people in various different parts of the world, popping up randomly though the years. Some postulated the bloodline was possibly part of an alien race. Other websites spoke about the direct connection to Adam and Eve from a Creation standpoint, "The immaculate humans are living proof that God exists, and that Creation is, in fact, true."

Other websites referred to the connection with the ancestral 'Eve,' an African ancestor all modern humans are supposedly descended from, some 200,000 years ago that scientists called the 'Mitochondrial Eve.' Was the extra rib part of the Mitochondrial Eve mutation, or was it simply an unrelated recessive trait?

I rolled up to grandma's care home where my mom was waiting for me just inside the entry. The home was named The Legion, a brown brick structure and nicely maintained yard space where several weeping willows that had lost their leaves. The gnarled, bowing trees created a canopy overhead, with one small apple tree beneath them. Rotten apples spotted the ground around the miniature tree, and as we got closer, I saw there was still one overripe apple left on the tree.

"Hi, Mom," I said. My mouth felt twitchy with my decision to go to Maryland, but I kept it shut.

"Hi, dear."

Next I felt a pang of guilt for not visiting Grandma in so long. It was increasingly difficult to visit, ever since she'd begun losing her short-term memory. The first time she'd forgotten my name was the worst, like a butter knife to the ribs. But now with Analiese gone, I had a whole new appreciation of family because I knew they could be wrenched from my fingertips at any moment.

Grandma Marion and Aunt Bethany were all we had left of Mom's side of the family. Mom's dad was dead, having died on a construction site when Mom was three years old. They were older parents when they had her, both in their mid-forties, and mom was their only child. Now, Grandma, Bethany, me and Mom were the only ones left.

Great-Aunt Bethany was Grandma's baby sister. She'd been a source of entertainment for years with her exaggerated innocence and dry wit. Dad always referred to her as a 'spinster' on account of the fact that she never married. The seventy-five year-old lived in Stonewood, and was still spry and active in her senior's community, as far as I knew.

A few steps in and we were at Grandma Marion's door. I knocked three times, hoping she would remember we were coming and be dressed appropriately, or... at least dressed.

She answered the door and her face drew up into a big smile I hoped was recognition.

"Hello my dears!" she said, hugging us. "Come in."

I exchanged a glance with Mom as we stepped into the small room Grandma called home. All that was left of the personal belongings of her life she shared with Grandpa was the intricately carved antique jewellery chest and two flowery blue sofas. Aunt Bethany was already seated in the living room. She reached out to greet us, since her hips prevented her from getting up off the couch without pain. "Hello!"

We greeted Aunt Bethany with hugs and kisses and sat down next to her on the sofa, Grandma joining us in the chair across the living area. Bethany was a slightly younger version of Grandma, with slightly darker hair, her complexion a tiny bit rosier.

"I'm so happy you could come today," Grandma said. "I've been thinking it must be time for you to visit." Grandma's mossy blue-green eyes were still as bright as ever. Her hair was grey along the sides, but the top and back were darker, the length of her hair tied up into a neat bun at the back of her head. No matter who or what she forgot in her life, be it her grandchildren or her boiling tea kettle, she somehow always remembered to wear her hair in a bun.

"I've been thinking so too, Grandma," I said. "How are you?" Would she even remember Analiese's death?

Grandma smiled. "Just fine, dear. Just fine." Obviously she'd forgotten about Analiese altogether. She turned to Mom. "And you?"

"We're both doing well," Mom said perfunctorily. Clearly she wasn't going to bring up Analiese and experience the fallout from the entire discussion. "We came to talk to you both about something important," Mom said.

"Oh?" Grandma glanced back and forth at us, her eyes wide, revealing yellowed whites.

"Adriana has been asking about the bloodline, and the extra rib," Mom said, launching in. "I remember hearing you and Aunt Bethany whispering about it once. What do you know about it?"

Grandma Marion merely blinked at first, her eyes unfocused as if her mind was in some faraway place. Then she snapped out of it and glanced at Bethany. "When I first heard about it, you were a new mother, Carla. You'd just given birth to Adriana and Analiese. I was introduced to a woman named Genevieve, about your age, who had an extra rib. I was told

Genevieve had the same rare blood type as my cousin's daughter, Virginia. No rhesus factor. Do you know what that is?"

"Rh factor refers to antigens, right?" I asked, not to clarify what I knew, but to confirm that grandma knew what she was talking about.

Grandma Marion nodded. "Antigens are what make the blood impure. Your blood has no antigens. No impurities. It is like O-negative, but yet it's not O-negative."

I still felt no more informed than I had when I walked through the door.

"What about her extra rib?" Mom continued to press Grandma.

"What other story in history talks about a rib?" Grandma prompted, eyebrows high on her forehead as she waited for us to figure it out.

My mind whirred. "Eve?"

Grandma Marion's face lit up into a wide grin, showing off long teeth. She nodded with enthusiasm and then all at once her face fell. My mother's complexion was an ashy shade of pale, her expression clouded over.

"You're not saying Adriana is... somehow connected to the Biblical Eve?" Mom asked.

"That is exactly what I'm telling you, dear," Grandma said.

Mom's pallor was still a chalky grey. "I think that assumption is going a bit too far, Mom."

Grandma held my mother's gaze. "I suppose only God would know for sure."

Thankfully, Aunt Bethany finally spoke up. "The strangest thing about that girl, Genevieve, with the extra rib and the blood type was that she could have been our Cousin Virginia's twin sister. I've never seen anyone resemble another person like that, especially when there's no blood relation. Their voices even sounded exactly the same. Do you remember that, Marion? Remember her dark hair and strange green eyes? Genevieve was the spitting image of Virginia."

"That's right," Grandma said. "Gosh, I almost forgot. Remember how we debated that for years after? We researched her family tree, trying to find a connection, a long lost relative we'd forgotten about. It was uncanny, how they looked exactly the same. Carbon copies."

"Did you find anything?" I asked.

Grandma wrung her hands in her lap. "No. Nothing. There were no relatives, not even distant. Genevieve said she was French, but we're all Scottish with only one English ancestor. Nobody in the family tree overlapped with Genevieve's. Not that we could find, anyway."

"Genevieve," I said. It sounded an awful lot like the extended version of Jennie or Jeannie.

Mom shook her head. "Why has nobody ever told me this before?"

Grandma Marion's face flushed pink, and her expression looked like she'd been caught stealing. "An omission of necessity, I suppose. When Virginia was alive, we thought we had to keep it a secret, even from our own family members. Government officials were speculating about the blood, wondering where in the world it came from. Of course, some crazies thought Virginia was an alien." Grandma frowned at the memory. "Once she realized she was so different, special, a kind of scientific curiosity, she tried to hide, disappear, for privacy, and for safety. She became a hermit those last few months of her life."

I stared at Grandma in a whole new light. "For safety? What were the safety risks?" I considered the experience I had with the National Human Genome Research Institute and their request that I stay for testing, followed by my mother's wacky response.

"The scientists."

"Scientists? Who? The Human Genome researchers?" I asked.

Grandma glanced to Bethany, who shrugged. "We're not sure."

It now seemed like an appropriate time to tell everyone about Kalan and Marcus. "I have something I think I'd better tell you all." I did so, explaining that they were here in search of their biological mother, who also had the blood type and the extra rib.

Auntie Bethany looked like she'd just gotten an incurable

diagnosis. "Oh, no. Marion, the worst has happened, hasn't it? They've found each other."

"Wait. What do you know about them?" I asked.

Grandma and Bethany locked gazes and something passed between them, an unspoken communication.

"The meeting between Genevieve and Virginia wasn't accidental," Aunt Bethany looked like she was about to cry, "This is where the story becomes complicated. When Virginia was twenty, she was considering getting married and had her blood taken. When it was typed, they placed it in the O-negative category. But as we all know, it isn't O-negative, is it?"

"No, it isn't," I said.

Bethany continued. "After that, they bothered Virginia to come to the Center for Inherited Disease Research for years and years. Eighteen years later, after numerous stillbirths and then her husband passing away, she finally had no reason to ignore their requests. She needed to know, once and for all, what in the world they wanted from her. That was the day she met Genevieve. Genevieve had been there for eight months."

"What does this have to do with Kalan and Marcus?" I asked. But I already knew the answer.

"She is the mother of those twins," said Aunt Bethany.

An icy shiver tiptoed up my back.

"I remember Genevieve!" Mom said, less of a question and more like she'd finally made the connection.

"Do you remember how much she looked like your second cousin, Virginia?" Grandma asked.

My mom nodded, her eyes glassy, absent.

"Poor Genevieve. And to top it all off, she was eight months pregnant with twins!" My heart thumped so loudly in my ears I barely heard the rest of what grandma said.

"How old was she? Genevieve?" I asked.

"Eighteen years old, I believe." Bethany replied.

"And they met eighteen years after Virginia had her blood typed?" I asked.

Grandma nodded. "That's right."

Virginia and Genevieve were eighteen years apart. Virginia was eighteen when she had her blood typed. They looked like carbon copies of one another. And yet, they weren't related, not even distantly. What were the odds?

"Genevieve was absolutely hysterical with fear," Bethany said. "She couldn't abort them. She tried, but it didn't work. Those demon babies refused to be terminated."

Demon babies. My skin crawled at the idea of Kalan having nearly been aborted. "Why did she try to abort them?"

"Because," Bethany answered. "Genevieve insisted she was impregnated while at the Centre. The scientists used her body for a scientific experiment. They used her body, like she was an animal. We figured they were trying to create a new breed."

A new breed. I swallowed back the lump in my throat.

"What did she do?"

"She came to live with us," Grandma said. "And spent the remainder of her pregnancy with Virginia, who took care of her, tried to keep her protected from those people. But Virginia couldn't protect her, and they both knew that. That's why they were so secretive, those two. They couldn't have been more like twins if they'd come out of the same womb. They had secrets they never told anybody, not even us. Those scientists already knew exactly where Virginia lived. She was being monitored, wire-tapped, everything."

Aunt Bethany nodded, then her eyes widened. "Adriana, is there a chance you are being monitored?" she asked.

"I...I don't know," I said.

"You'd better watch out." Bethany warned. Grandma bobbed her head in agreement.

"What about Uncle Les? Did he know about all of this?" I asked, referring to their younger brother, my sister's assaulter. The black sheep of the family.

Bethany's eyes clouded over. "He knows. But don't get involved with him. You know what he's like."

"But would he know anything about where Genevieve went?" I asked.

"No!" My mother said with a wild expression. Her mouth clamped shut.

Bethany agreed. "Les can't be trusted. After what he did to

your sister... Well, he's a despicable man. He's not right in the head." She tapped her temple.

I cringed at the thought of Les, the old pervert who felt Analiese up when she was only twelve. The fact that Analiese was now dead only intensified my feelings of hate toward the nasty pedophile.

"What happened to the babies?" I already knew the answer, but I wanted to know what they would say.

"Genevieve gave those unnatural babies away," Auntie Bethany said. "Sent them away, and she went into hiding."

Mom's eyes flashed, her nostrils flaring. "Where did she go?"

"We never heard of her again. Not once did she try to contact us. Not once did she call. She disappeared. Fell off the face of the earth. After a while, we tried to forget about her. It seemed safer that way." Aunt Bethany looked at grandma, and they nodded in agreement.

"Safer. Why?" I asked.

Aunt Bethany's eyes darkened. "Because Virginia died two weeks before those babies were born. From 'unknown causes.'"

I swallowed. "And you think...?"

Now it was Auntie Bethany's expression that was dark. "They killed her. The scientists murdered our Virginia."

#

Immediately, Mom and I went to her house and I got on the

phone with the Department of the Coroner. On the other end of the line was a snotty sounding woman who was clearly annoyed I'd interrupted her internet surfing. I explained to her that I needed a historical Coroner's report and gave her Virginia's name.

"You will need to written authorization to release the report about this person." I could have sworn I heard some humor in her voice. "And there are some fees associated with this service."

I rolled my eyes. "Okay. Virginia MacLean has been dead quite a while. Next of kin may be difficult to track down."

There was silence on the line for moment. "Those are the laws. I don't make them."

"Look," I kept my voice steady, "I'm a relative, and I'm inquiring into a genetic condition in our family. There must be some way of accessing that report."

"There are ways of accessing that report. Next of kin, usually a spouse, a parent or a child can sign the authorization."

I pressed the mute button on the phone. "Mom, they say next of kin can sign for the report."

Mom shrugged. "Grandma Marion or Bethany are all that's left."

I released the Mute button. "Ma'am, the only next of kin are elderly cousins, do they count?"

She sighed, as if my question was absurd. "Obviously."

Finally, some headway.

#

I picked up Grandma Marion and went straight to the Coroner's office where we came into contact with the woman who I'd spoken to on the telephone. She looked nothing like I expected. She was well over forty, with spiked burgundy-blue hair and a bare face.

"We are here for Virginia MacLean's autopsy report. This is Marion Rask, her next of kin." I asked.

Grandma smiled at the woman. "Hello."

She looked at me and grandma with a blank expression. "Can I get your documentation, please?"

"Sure," Grandma placed her huge, wobbly brown purse on the desk and began to dig through it. She pulled out her birth certificate, which was clearly a modern reprint, judging by the bright colors. She handed it to the woman. "Here you go."

The woman peered at the document and then set it beside her keyboard. Next, she had us fill out a form with as much demographic data about Virginia as we knew. "Okay. I'll see what I can find…" She clicked her mouse as she watched her computer monitor, her gaze flicking around the screen. "Found it." She looked up at me, her face impassive.

I looked back. "Can I get it?"

"There's a fifty dollar processing fee," she said.

*For Christ's sake.* When would this get easy? I dug my credit card out of my wallet and held it out for her.

She took my credit card, ran it through her machine, and

once my receipt was ready, she went into a locked back room. When she returned, she was holding a manila folder. "Would you like a photocopy?"

"Yes, please."

She removed the staples from the document, ran it through the photocopier, and then handed them to me. They were warm and smelled like fresh ink.

"Thank you," I said. "Come on, Grandma," I laced my arm through her elbow and we walked out. Once in my car, I began to examine the document.

"What does it say, dear?" Grandma asked.

"Patient died of unknown causes," I read out loud. I continued reading, watching for details about Virginia's anatomy. There was a cursory comment on the blood type and how it was likely due to lab error. Further down the report it was noted that she had a surgical scar at the bottom of her abdomen, where, *it appears the patient had some sort of surgical procedure involving the ribcage, based on the scar tissue along the top row of ribs. While there is some evidence of a possible former presence of a supernumerary rib, however, there are currently twenty-four intact ribs.*"

Had Virginia's extra rib been removed? If so, why?

*Then the Lord said to Cain, "Where is your brother Abel?"*
*"I don't know," he replied. "Am I my brother's keeper?"*
*-Genesis 4:9, The Holy Bible*

## CHAPTER SIX

### ADRIANA SINCLAIR

I went to Kalan's hotel following my review of the Coroner's report. Marcus was gone, out to get food, and Kalan stayed behind to make a list of places to go in Stonewood, places that could lead to clues about his mother. Kalan sat in an armchair and I sat on the bed across from him. He set his cell phone down on the table.

"I'm putting off my trip to Maryland for now," I said.

"Why?"

"I don't feel like going yet. I want to help you with your mother, first. Obviously there is a connection here. Between us."

"Are you sure? It's pretty important for you to go."

I shook my head. It wasn't just because of Kalan's mother. I wasn't sure if I could cope with being alone in Maryland for any length of time. I was deluding myself to think I could actually be that independent at this point in my life. The admission of such a weakness, even to myself, angered me. But there was also the matter of trying to figure out what the hell happened to Virginia, and how it related to Kalan's mother. I latched onto it. A much less needy reason not to go.

"I think I know something about what happened to your mother." The words spilled from my mouth, not at all subtle. Damn it.

His eyes widened. "Really?"

I swallowed on the lump in my throat. "I think your mother was used for an experiment. I think maybe you and Marcus are a result of that experiment."

Kalan's mouth dropped open. He looked at me for several seconds before he finally responded, as if his mind was searching for words that evaded him. His eyes narrowed. "What makes you think that?"

"Why are you here? Be honest. Why did you seek me out? It's not just because you wanted to find your mother, is it?"

A hurt look passed over Kalan's face, but it was gone so fast I wondered if I'd seen it at all. "It sounds to me like you've got a theory. Why don't you tell me?"

"My grandmother thinks scientists impregnated your mother," I said.

Kalan turned away and muttered. I'd never heard him swear before and I found it somewhat startling. His eyes were hard, imperious. Like brushed steel. "What else did she say?"

I explained everything Grandma and Aunt Bethany told me about Virginia and Genevieve.

"They knew my mother?" Kalan asked, his voice was almost breathless.

"Yes." I hesitated. "And there's something else. Two weeks before you and Marcus were born, Virginia died. She was in her late thirties."

Kalan chewed his lip. "What do I do now? Your Grandma's Cousin dies two weeks before my mother has us, gives us up and then takes off. Who's left to ask now? Anybody?"

An idea came to me, a reprehensible, vile idea that I barely wanted to allow space within my mind, let alone say the thought out loud.

"I have an estranged uncle," I started, "He's a total asshole child molester... but he might know something."

"Did he hurt you?" Kalan's eyes glittered like shards of glass.

"No. Analiese was his chosen victim." My chin quivered. I covered it with my hand.

Kalan swore under his breath. "Do you know where he lives?"

It had been a long time, but Les's dingy apartment was still firm in my memory. "Yes. I'll never forget that creepy little dungeon he calls home."

"Do you think he'll tell us anything?" Kalan asked. With

the light coming in through the window beside him, his satiny eyelashes were lit up.

"Doubtful."

"Let's try anyway," Kalan's silvery gaze momentarily locked on mine. A strange stirring built deep in my stomach, like thousands of butterflies had been released.

"Thanks. For coming with me," I said. "I don't think I could face him alone."

Kalan nodded. We got into his car and drove in silence toward the suburb where my great-uncle lived. It felt like a lifetime ago that Analiese died, like I'd been without her forever. I yearned for the past, before her accident, before I met Kalan or learned I was... different. Now, everything had changed, and I no longer knew which way was up.

Kalan's gentle voice broke into my thoughts. "Hey. You're pretty quiet over there. Is everything okay?"

How should I answer? Was everything okay? Had I come to terms with the myriad of strange information I'd learned in the past several weeks? With the death of my twin? *Twinkilled. No. I'm not okay. I will never be okay again.*

"I don't know. It's a lot to take in. No."

"It is," Kalan said. "Are you bothered by the idea that I'm an experiment?"

The words hung in the air between us. "I'm not bothered, Kalan. You are what you are. You're a good person. It isn't our genes that determine who we are, it's our actions." Kalan didn't respond, but I knew by his half smile he was satisfied. "The only thing we have going for us is this lead," I said.

Kalan pursed his lips together, and when he parted them again, they'd turned white, the pink returning to them slowly. *Stop looking at him like that.* I looked away.

"You're right," Kalan said. "Next stop, Uncle Les."

The remainder of the drive I drifted in and out of an overwrought sleep.

*Marcus stood before me, his body morphing first to shiny black stone, like a statue made of obsidian. He shattered apart into grains of black sand and then to smoke; a whirl wind spinning, slowly at first but growing faster and faster. Kalan appeared to my right, and he seemed to glow, as if lit up from the inside out. The whirling blackness of Marcus inched toward Kalan, the tendrils of smoke whipping out like talons. Each time there was contact, Kalan was sliced horizontally, his pale body oozing crimson blood. Kalan held out his hand, as if extending it for a handshake. One black wisp stretched and Kalan grasped it, and in a flash of blinding white light, the whirling blackness that was Marcus was gone. Kalan stood there, slices ringing his body every half inch, blood dripping onto the floor. Four round dots of blood on the floor, evenly spaced...*

A piercing scream woke me up. Sitting bolt upright, I opened my eyes to see the road stretched out in front of me.

"What's wrong?" Kalan slammed on the brakes and I lurched forward. With lightning reflexes he reached out, placing his arm across my chest to protect me from hitting the dashboard as he pulled over to the side of the road, his eyes wide. How could he move so fast?

I took a deep breath. "A nightmare. Just a nightmare."

"Are you okay?" Kalan asked.

The landscape out the passenger side window brought me back to the here and now. Instantly, I knew by the carefully planted elms staggered every five feet, I was on the street that led to Uncle Les's senior's home.

"How is this going to go?" I asked.

Kalan parked the car. "Who knows? Bad?"

"He's not going to cooperate," I said.

"We'll see."

I shivered at the way Kalan said those words, *We'll see*, so matter-of-factly. He'd always been so gentle, but I was beginning to realize there was more to Kalan than his angelic good looks.

We went into the senior's home and as we neared his apartment, my heart began to stutter. By the time we reached the door I was certain Kalan could hear the pounding.

Kalan rapped on the door three times. A barking voice answered. "Who's there?"

"It's your niece, Adriana," I called out. Nasty old fuck. There was a moment of hesitation before the chain latch was slid across, followed by the dead bolt turning.

The door creaked as he opened the door only wide enough to poke his head out. "Oh. You."

My palms dripped sweat. This was the man who molested Analiese when she was only twelve years old. He opened the door the rest of the way, wide enough to finally see Kalan. Then he froze, stock-still, his mouth half-open.

"I'm here to ask you some questions," I said through gritted teeth. I could hardly keep my voice from wavering. "This is my friend, Kalan."

Uncle Les's brows lowered and he gave Kalan a quick once-over. Then he grunted and opened the door. His near-black hair hadn't been trimmed for some time and also clearly hadn't been washed, the way it stuck up in greasy points around his head. His green eyes had turned a mossy hue from the veil of cataracts that covered them. His teeth were yellowed from years of cigarette smoking, his skin reddened and criss-crossed with wrinkles like boot leather.

Les walked back into his apartment. "Well, are you coming in or not?"

I shoved my sweaty, shaking hands into my pockets and glanced at Kalan, whose grim expression told me he wasn't impressed. We went in.

My skin crawled. Uncle Les had every window covered, the curtains drawn. The space was dimly lit with one tiny lamp in the corner of the room. It served to highlight the eerie quality of the space with drab furnishings and washed-out colours. The entire palette was in shades of beige and gray. The smell of stale smoke and dirty laundry turned my stomach. The weighted door shut behind us and eclipsed all remaining natural light, so that we were plunged into a dingy, smoke-filled dungeon.

"Why are you here?" Uncle Les asked. No attempt at social niceties.

I drew in a breath. "Genevieve. Do you remember that name?" I waited a minute to see if he'd respond, but he didn't. "Auntie Bethany and Grandma do. I bet you do too. I was hoping you could tell us what you know about her."

Les's eyes narrowed. "It don't matter if I remember or not. Why would I tell you a goddamn thing?" He pointed at me with his lit cigarette, the smouldering end bright red, a tiny weapon. The round white scar on Analiese's left arm flashed through my mind. Fucking. Asshole.

My voice wavered as I failed to contain my temper. "You don't say anything about Analiese dying? You can't answer a simple question, even if my safety depends on it?" I was speaking far too loud in the enclosed space.

Les chortled. More of a hoot, really. "You come in here with your damn white bodyguard," he gestured to Kalan with his cigarette hand, "and try to guilt trip me? You've got another thing coming, girlie."

With two steps I closed the space between us and backhanded Les's cheek. A funny sound sputtered from him and his eyes went wide. Then a smile crept across his face, his teeth yellowed and long. "That all you got?"

"No." I slapped him again, this time, my whole open hand across his cheek, the base of my palm coming into contact with his jaw. Teeth clattered inside his mouth, sending a vibration through to the skin of my hand. His head spun to the side from the impact and then went back, like a globe teetering on its axis. "That's still not all. Want more?"

Les was no longer smiling. "What the hell do you want?"

Kalan's spine straightened, ready to defend me. But all Uncle Les did was sit down on the sofa next to the lamp and set his cigarette in an ashtray, a thin thread of smoke rising from it, creating curlicues that rose up into the lamp shade. Once he settled his ass into the sofa, he grabbed the cigarette and took a drag from it, staring straight ahead as if Kalan and I weren't even there.

I strode across the room and sat down adjacent to Uncle Les. Kalan remained standing, coiled and ready, as if he would pounce across the room at my word.

"Les. After everything you've done, don't you think you owe me this much?"

He glared at me, his eyes slotted, his nose flared. He refused to respond.

"Here is your chance to make things right and tell me what

you know. You have no reason to keep it from me."

"I want compensation. I'm an old man. All I got is my old age security. I want money." His gruff voice was gravelly, from too many years of chain-smoking. "And don't you try to guilt-trip me. That little slut of a sister—"

I launched myself from my chair and backhanded him as hard as I could. His face rocketed to the side from the impact and his mouldy eyes widened in disbelief. "Don't you talk about Analiese that way you fucking pedophile!" The back of my hand stung and my wrist throbbed. *I could so easily kill you right now, old man.*

"Bitch," Les muttered under his breath, rubbing his bright red cheek. He pointed with his cigarette hand, right at Kalan. "Is he one of 'em?"

"One of...?"

"Genevieve's oddball twins."

My cheeks flooded with heat. He knew. "He is."

"He don't look nothing like her. I guess sometimes those family genes get all screwed up, don't they?" Les looked at me, a creepy smile tugging at the corners of his face. "Except for you and Analiese. You look just like your daddy, don't you?"

My blond-haired, blue eyed dad popped into my mind. He was the ultimate California boy. He couldn't have been more opposite of me and Analiese, with our nearly black hair and green eyes. "What the hell are you talking about, you old fool?"

Les snorted and took another drag from his super-heated cigarette. "What? Your mom never told you who your real daddy is?"

My stomach turned to lead, my heart heavy in my chest. He wasn't implying...

A chuckle erupted from his mouth. He obviously saw something in my expression that amused him. "I think you're catching on now, aren't you? You're pretty smart. Just like yer old man."

It couldn't be. The possibility was too vile to consider. Dr. McGill's words flitted through my mind, unbidden. *"Homozygous are recessive traits. They're typically inherited when both parents are carriers of the traits. Their father must have the majority of recessive traits."*

Recessive traits. Homozygous traits. Traits found in blood relatives.

Kalan's hand on my arm brought me back to the horrific reality of this situation. "Are you okay?" he asked.

I shook my head, unable to answer, my thoughts racing, my emotions flinging around in my body like a wild ferret looking for a weakness in its cage.

"I have to leave," I managed to squeak out. My stomach turned and threatened the back of my throat. Bitter bile filled my mouth.

"What's wrong?" Les guffawed. "You mad at your mom

for lying to you all these years?"

With that, Kalan set off across the room, his long legs carrying him to Uncle Les in less than three strides. Les startled and jumped backward against the sofa. He dropped his smoke into his lap, but stared at Kalan for a beat before fishing it out from between his legs.

Kalan's voice was low and menacing. "I'm not interested in hearing you goad Adriana for one more second. The pain you have caused her and her family is enough. I can't begin to understand what the hell is wrong with you that you have chosen to do these things, hurting people for your own selfish desires, and I don't really care to know. But you will give us the information we came here for. And if you don't tell us, I will take the information from you. Voluntary or by force. It's your choice."

A strange sensation unfolded deep in my belly. A twisting feeling. Like my body was about to internally combust and I'd suddenly become millions of ashes, floating, directionless.

"I'll tell you what you want," Les said, sliding forward on his grungy sofa and then pushing himself to standing. "Just a sec. I have something I want to show ya." He left the room.

Kalan and I looked at one another. Was he really going to give it up to us? Was it really going to be that easy?

I heard a click. Followed by a creak of hinges. Shit.

"Help me! Help. Help. Somebody. I need help." Les's voice rang down the hall of the home.

"Let's go." I got up, and Kalan followed suit.

We went to the door just as a security guard reached Les's door way. The middle aged guard had a receding hairline and his beer belly spilled over the top of his blue uniform pants, his blue shirt stretched wide and gaping at the buttons to reveal a little bit of hairy stomach. His baggy skin looked like he should smell like stale cigarettes and old coffee, but instead, he smelled like expensive aftershave.

Kalan and I stepped out of the suite to see Les pointing at us, his expression all bunched up and twisted, a pathetic attempt at looking fearful. Bastard.

"Those two. They're threatening me!" Les said, maintaining his wide eyed, scared old man look while the guard's gaze was on him, his expression transforming into amusement as soon as the guard looked at us. He actually even stifled a chuckle.

"What are you doing here, bothering Mr. Les, here?" The guard obviously didn't even know his full name.

"He's my uncle," I said, barely able to contain the need to slap that self-righteous smile right off of Les's face. "My friend and I are trying to find someone he knows. He doesn't feel like telling us. He's just being stubborn."

The guard looked at my uncle. "Is this true, Les?"

"Nah. They're trying to force me to tell them things they have no business knowin'."

The guard set his hand on his waist, where a radio was held

on to a utility belt. "I think you should leave now."

"But, Les. Why won't you tell us?" I took a step toward the lech but the guard stepped directly in front of me, blocking my access.

"That's enough, Miss."

Protecting a pedophiliac old bastard. I was pretty sure the guard had absolutely no idea who Les was, or what he'd done. If he did, it would be highly doubtful he'd be working so hard to protect the prick.

"Fine. We'll leave." I looked back at Kalan who eyed Les with an icy gaze. Les seemed to shrink back, just a bit.

The guard escorted us out, Les watching us every step of the way. He nodded right before we stepped out of view.

#

Back in the car, my head swam with thoughts of what I'd just heard. We left the parking lot of Les's home, only to pull into the nearest back ally where we could watch the building and Les from a distance. A distance far enough that Mr. Rire-A-Cop couldn't see us.

"What did you mean when you said you'd take the information voluntarily or by force?" I asked.

Kalan shrugged. "I was hoping a little threat might make him talk."

I nodded. Using the threat of physical force never occurred to me because I knew they were empty threats. I just hit. Not that it worked. Les was all but unfazed by my slaps.

I took in a breath and my thoughts turned to something even viler than slapping the creepy old man.

"Homozygous traits," I said, my voice oddly flat. "That's why the scientist wanted to run tests on my biological father. That's why my mother was so sketchy. She didn't want me to know."

"God, I'm so sorry," Kalan said.

I couldn't even look at Kalan right now. "Recessive traits that both parents pass down to their offspring. Do you know who has recessive traits? Yeah. Relatives. That's who."

I started to cry then, tears streaming down my face, re-igniting sore cheeks that had been exposed to salty tears for far too many days in a row. At what point did tears run out? At what point would I stop feeling like I was stepping from one nightmare into another and another, only to find out I would never wake up?

I hardly even noticed when Kalan gathered me up into his arms. I buried my face in his chest, and let the tears flow. There was nothing left in my life that I'd once known to be true. Not even my own parents were who they seemed. Kalan was the one and only person I felt like I could count on, and I'd only known him for a few days. I missed Analiese so much my bones ached with it.

After what must have been over thirty minutes of me crying in his arms and the silence of the interior of the car magnifying every single gasp, Kalan finally spoke. "Genetics aren't everything.

My foster parents and siblings are more my family than Marcus will ever be. He may be your biological father, but he is not your dad. And if he molested your sister, it is more than likely he did the same to your mother."

I hadn't even reached that conclusion yet. I was so fixated on my mother's lie I didn't even stop to consider why she might be lying. Had he sexually abused her, too? I counted the months back from my parents' marriage and our birth date. Analiese and I had been born in May. Our parents were married in December. Five months. She definitely conceived us prior to their wedding. A shotgun wedding. Now my mother's young age at marriage— seventeen—seemed far less romantic and more horrifying. As a young girl, I'd always believed they got married young because they were madly in love and about to have a baby. Following their divorce, I rearranged my belief to be about misguided, stupid teenagers.

Maybe they got married because she was pregnant with her uncle's children.

Or was Uncle Les up to his usual tricks of mind games and manipulation? Either was plausible. Lies were all part of Les's MO, and he seemed to take particular pleasure in messing around with people's emotions. He got off on it. Sick old fuck.

I had to stop thinking about it. It was a question that wouldn't be answered tonight, and I was partially relieved that it wasn't, because I couldn't quite face the possibility that my uncle was my father. It was just too... sick.

The natural light around us was fading as day turned to evening. My stomach started to growl so I pulled a couple of granola bars from my purse. I offered one to Kalan who took it willingly. As we ate, the front doors of Les's building opened. It was Les. He waved at the Rent-A-Cop and set off down the road. He walked right into the entrance to the back alley, and he would have seen us had he looked, but his expression was of a man with a destination in firm in his mind.

"Should we follow him?" I asked.

Kalan answered by putting the car in gear. He inched forward to the street where the nose of the vehicle stuck out only far enough for us to see Les. We got there just in time to see him turn down a side street. Kalan followed, swallowing back his granola bar as quickly as he could.

"Where the hell is the skinner going?" Kalan muttered as he peered down the next block. Les was definitely a man on a mission. He walked a lot faster than I would have thought he was capable.

Then he turned to his right and ducked out of view.

"Shit." Kalan sped off in that direction, but all that was around were a series of small bungalows that appeared to have built in the 1940's. The houses were dark, all except for one. As we inched up the street, I noted how the yards were unkempt. One was littered with animal feces. The next yard's grass was overrun with weeds and thistle, the bright purple flowers blooming even in fall. The final yard, the one with the light on, was littered with cigarette butts, beer bottles and various kinds of refuse: a Styrofoam cup, a gum wrapper, an empty pack of cigarettes.

"Look." I pointed to the window where people could be seen moving about inside. Immediately, Les's ugly mug came into view.

"There he is," Kalan said. "What's he doing in there?"

We waited until another face moved into our line of sight. First, a woman. Then, a child.

"There's a kid in there!" I said. My heart was in my throat, pounding. What was he doing here? Who was the woman? And what about the child? I couldn't breathe. This child was at risk and I couldn't be witness to Les destroying another life. I opened the car door.

"What are you doing?" Kalan reached out and grasped my arm, preventing me from getting out of the car. It was a gentle grip, but oddly firm. Too firm.

I looked back at the window. Les was now sitting down, smoking a cigarette, a beer bottle on the table in front of him. "I need to warn them."

Just then, the woman pointed at Les and the little girl rounded the table and sat down on his knee. I pulled from Kalan's grasp and got out the car, careful to close the door with a light touch. I didn't want to alert the bastard. He wasn't going to get a head start.

Kalan got out and fell into step beside me as I approached the door. Without knocking, I walked in, Kalan behind me.

Immediately I came face to face with Les, a scruffy little girl on his lap, and a woman across the table from him.

The child looked to be about nine years old, her mouse-brown hair shoulder length, greasy at the roots. Her complexion was pale, except for the dark bags under her eyes. She was underweight, her bony knees jutting out from beneath her ripped orange shirtdress. But it was her eyes that haunted me the most. Beautiful blue eyes that looked at me with a kind of hollowness I'd never before seen in a child. A look of complete and utter detachment.

Les pushed her off his knee with a forceful shove. "What the hell..?" He stood up, the child looking up at him and at me, eyes blank. The woman cowered in her sitting position at the table, her hands shaking. Even her frizzy bleached hair wiggled with her trembling.

"Do you know this man is a child molester?" I asked as I walked toward him, my finger pointed. "Are you aware he likes to sexually abuse young girls?"

"Get the hell out of here, bitch." Les's voice was a low, hissing growl. Smoke swirled out of his mouth as he spoke, lending an even more sinister look to his curled back lips.

I spoke to the woman, who refused to look me in the eye.

"He molested my sister. He ruined her life. I thought you should know that."

"Get out." Les said.

The child stepped away from us and sat down on the floor where a tiny doll lay in a miniature baby crib. She picked it up and held it to her chest.

"What are you doing here, uncle? Are you going to hurt that little girl, too?"

"Aaah!" Les yelled, his face red as a tomato. He lunged at me but Kalan stepped in his way, blocking Les's access. Les bounced off of Kalan and stumbled backward, his ass coming down on the table. It upended, sending the cigarettes, ashtrays, roll-your-own papers and tobacco to the floor, Les half sitting, half laying on them. The woman held her lit cigarette in the air, staring at the spectacle before her like she couldn't quite believe it. Les scrabbled to his feet.

"Remember when I said you had a choice, tell me about my mother willingly, or have it taken from you by force?" Kalan asked.

Les didn't respond.

"Well, the time has come old man," Kalan said. "Make your decision."

"You're going to take it, are ya? Try it, because that's the only way you're going to get it out of me, weirdo."

Kalan's hands were on Uncle Les's face so fast, the

movement reminded me of the way a snake attacked its prey. Les's mouth dropped open the moment Kalan looked him in the eye.

Les's voice came out in a string of high-pressured, toneless words. "Last I saw her she was in Denver, in the slums. She's living on the street, People know her as Jenny. I took a picture of her. It's in the bottom of my top dresser drawer."

Kalan turned to me and nodded.

"Give us your keys," I said.

Les reached around and pulled a set of keys from his back pocket. They were on a keychain that had an image attached to it, an image contained in a hard layer of plastic. It was of my mother, me and Analiese. My stomach felt like a block of ice.

"You have ten minutes, Lester," Kalan said, letting go of the man. "And then you go home and forget about this nice lady and her daughter."

Les nodded and the woman just stared. The little girl didn't look up from the floor, her baby and crib clutched tightly to her chest.

We walked to the car in complete silence. When I got in, I stared at the dash for several minutes, the atmosphere between us so tense it was palpable.

"What the hell just happened in there?" I asked.

Kalan's posture drooped and he swallowed. "Okay. I need to tell you something. I don't expect you to believe this, but I'm going to tell you anyway." He held my gaze. "You already know

I'm searching for answers to my existence. It's clear we're from a genetic line of... well, something different. But there's something you don't know."

I held my breath.

"Marcus and I are different. You can see the physical stuff, with me being albino," Kalan looked down. "But there's more."

Silence passed between us. Finally, after what felt like a long, awkward moment, I broke the silence. "Continue."

Kalan let out a noisy exhale. "We have qualities about us that aren't normal... we have abilities that are beyond the average human."

I sat there, unsure what to say. How do you possibly respond to a declaration like that?

Kalan continued. "Marcus and I can do things."

"Do things," I said slowly. "Like, what kinds of things?"

"He's always instinctively known how to tap into certain abilities, to get what he wants. It hasn't been like that for me. While he seemed to know what to do, apparently even as a kid, my abilities came and went randomly and I had no control. It didn't help that I didn't want to accept the truth of what I was. I wanted to be normal." His last words come out gravelly.

"I still have no idea what you're referring to, Kalan. What are these things, these abilities Marcus possesses?"

"To begin with, we are both very strong. Stronger than normal. Marcus has more strength and speed than any other person

I've ever met. But there's more. Actually, I don't even know of everything he can do." Kalan's forehead creased, perhaps in embarrassment? "He's revealing it to me slowly. I don't think he totally trusts me yet. I can only assume that is true because I don't trust him yet, either."

My head pounded. "You must be aware of at least one of those abilities, besides strength?"

"Marcus has psychic abilities. He can manipulate thoughts, control people."

"Jesus." My head felt twice its normal size. "How do you know for sure?"

"We're staying at that hotel for free."

"Holy shit," I said. *This is crazy.*

"The truth is stranger than fiction when it comes to the two of us." Kalan paused for a beat, and then continued. "My abilities are more complicated, more... touchy. I wish I could tap into them the way Marcus does. But he's spent his entire life working on it, practicing. I've been so busy trying to convince myself I was normal and living in denial I've lost valuable time I could have used trying to figure it all out."

"What abilities do you have that you are you aware of?" *And he could leap tall buildings in a single bound...*the thought flitted through my mind, unbidden, of Kalan in a blue and red costume, cape flapping in the wind.

Kalan ran a hand through his hair, and the strands fell back down like silver threads of gossamer silk. "I don't have full-on mind control like Marcus, but I do have the ability to influence others' thoughts, to manipulate them. The first time was when I was eight years old and my foster mother brought me with her to the grocery store. I was intent on getting a toy soldier. I begged for her to buy it for me. She repeatedly said no but I wouldn't stop badgering her. Finally, after she threatened to punish me, I grew quiet, but inside I was screaming at her with my mind. I thought the same thing over and over: 'You will buy me the soldier! You will!' Then the strangest thing happened. She stopped dead in her tracks, turned to me with a big smile and said, 'I bet you'd like that toy soldier, wouldn't you Kalan?' But as soon as I realized I could do it I felt so guilty. I thought I was an evil child. I thought that if others found out, they would know how bad I was. So I went out of my way trying to deny it and pretended it never happened. Only recently have I attempted to use it again. But only if I need to. Like with Les."

I sucked in a deep breath, my mind whirling. "You control people's thoughts."

"I manipulate thoughts. I can't control them, not like Marcus can."

"Semantics. You affect what other people think, and therefore, you can make them do things they wouldn't normally do."

Kalan's mouth dropped open. "If you're thinking I would do

something to you, without your permission, I wouldn't."

"Would I even know the difference?"

He considered this for a moment. "I guess you wouldn't. But I'm asking you to put some faith in me, to trust me when I say I wouldn't do that to you. Ever."

Was this feeling I had toward him, this empathy and understanding, was it really me? Was I in control of my own thoughts and feelings right now? I felt like myself, like my thoughts were a result of my own free volition. If this was mind manipulation, it didn't feel like it. The feelings I had for him felt genuine, I was certain. "Okay."

Kalan's lips pursed together. "Are you horrified?"

Was I horrified? I wasn't sure. I hesitated.

"I need to know, because I don't want you to think negative things about me. I don't want you to be reviled by me."

I swallowed. "Why is my opinion of you so important?" I asked.

He shrugged. "I don't know."

"You just met me. You hardly even know me at all." I said.

Kalan covered his mouth with his hand. "I know. I can't explain it because I don't understand it. All I know is that when I'm around you, it's like...everything changes. What was once dull and boring is now exciting and vivid. What was once typical and mundane is like a brand-new experience. I like how I feel when I'm around you. Like I'm finally alive."

My heart skipped a beat. Did I feel the same way? "I don't know what to say."

"You don't need to say anything," he said.

A few moments of awkward silence passed between us. "Does Marcus control people all the time or just sometimes?"

"It seems Marcus uses it only as needed. If he meets resistance."

I thought of him, Zoe and Tait last night. "Did he use it on Tait or Zoe? To convince them to help him find your mother?"

"No, I don't think so. He prefers consent," Kalan said. "It's easier, because people are more lucid, more useful. He's more likely to use it if he's meeting serious barriers. Like no money and nowhere to stay. It's not that important for hotel staff to remember minute details. They merely need to hand us a key card and we're set."

I imagined Marcus hovering over some poor young hotel clerk and muttering, *You are getting so very sleepy...*

"I know Marcus can control thoughts, but do you have any personal examples of it? Have you seen him do it? What's it like?"

Kalan took a deep breath. "When Marcus initially entered my life, I was ecstatic that I had real, flesh-and-blood relatives. It's a foster child's dream come true to have a real family. But my happiness was short-lived. Marcus has quite a mean streak. Probably because of how he was treated at home." Kalan glanced at me. "He was always trying to tempt me to get into mischief with him. It started with pranks, leaving snakes in the bathtub, cockroaches in beds. As time went on, his pranks grew strange and malicious. A dead bird in my foster sister's bed."

"Christ," I muttered. "If he was killing birds and scaring children when he was fifteen and sixteen, what is he capable of now?"

"He's capable of anything. I believe that."

Now I understood the tenuous relationship between Kalan and his brother. He may be his only known blood relative but that didn't mean he could trust him.

"We should go," I said.

Kalan merely nodded, his posture tense as he drove to Les's apartment building. On the way, I called the emergency crisis line and provided the address of the home we'd just left. I stated the child looked like she needed medical treatment, then I hung up.

At Les's place, we avoided the Rent-A-Cop at the front entrance and found a back door. It was luckily only a few feet from Les's apartment and we were able to get in without being seen by any residents.

I went to his bedroom and rummaged through the drawer, enduring the smell of stale laundry and dirty old man. When my fingers touched the edge of the paper photo, I pulled it out of the drawer and quickly glanced at it. It was a woman with vivid teal eyes. Just like mine. I left the disgusting bedroom.

Kalan was already standing at the entryway, holding the door open for me. I handed him the photo.

"Will he remember what you did to him?" I asked.

Kalan shook his head. "No."

We exited the dungeon-like apartment. I welcomed the light of the hallway.

The fact that this was the first time Kalan had seen what his own mother looked like was completely eclipsed by the fact that I'd just learned my whole entire life had been one, giant lie.

I couldn't think about it anymore. "Does your mother look the way you thought she would?"

"No. She looks...miserable." Kalan handed the photo to me. The woman was lying on the sidewalk in her sleeping bag, a raincoat done up tightly around her head. All that showed was her pale, drawn face with dark shadows under her eyes and hollows below her cheekbones. But her eyes blazed, even from within the photograph, the colour of them as bright as laser-cut jewels. While her colouring was nothing like Kalan or Marcus, it was obvious she was their mother. Her high cheekbones, full lips and arched brows were exactly the same as theirs. Even in this photo, living as a street bum, covered in layers of dirt, she was extraordinarily beautiful. I'd seen this face before, in a photograph. It was the same as... Virginia's face.

Kalan stared straight ahead, blinking. Were his eyes moist?

"I'm sorry. This must be so painful," I said.

Kalan shook his head. "It's just that... I suppose I never believed it was possible to find her. The thought of her was always so idealized in my mind. To see the reality of the situation now, the starkness of it..."

"I know." I placed my hand on Kalan's arm. "Let's go find your mother."

*Even though identical twins supposedly share all of their DNA,*
*they acquire hundreds of genetic changes early in development*
*that could set them on different paths, according to new research.*
*-Live Science*

## CHAPTER SEVEN

### KALAN KANE

"Look at this sign in the photo," Adriana said. She was referring to a side of a building, a red brick wall painted white with blue lettering that was half worn off. "It looks like it says Matinees, or… something. I bet we can find it online. Just a sec." She began typing madly into her phone with her thumbs, "It says the old Matinees Hotel is on 48th Street and Duke. Do you think she could still be in that area?"

"It's worth a try," I said.

I turned onto the interstate that led straight into Denver. Once there we went straight into one of the most dangerous areas of the city. I shook off the jitters that crawled all over my skin. I had to find my mother.

"I feel terrible for dragging you here with me. It's not safe for you, or anyone else." My voice was thick and strained.

"We'll be fine. We have locks on the doors," Adriana said, her jaw set.

Miles later, we entered downtown Denver and eventually took the exit that led us to Duke Street. Another three blocks brought us to 48th Street, where the hotel sat on the corner, boarded up and abandoned. Driving by the barricaded main entrance, I turned the car and entered the darkened back alley. My courage waned as I looked at this terrible place, where human misery and suffering was at its most wretched.

I slowed down. People lay scattered about, sleeping on bare concrete, litter strewn everywhere, their possessions in shopping carts or plastic bags beside them. Some individuals had tarps for protection, for shade from the sun and rain, while others hid under trees and makeshift shanty-houses fashioned with wood and scraps of material.

The alley itself was part asphalt, part gravel, dumpsters and garbage cans staggered amongst the people. The crumbling brick walls of the back of the buildings were spoiled further with graffiti, and spindly trees were so overgrown they hung down into the roadway and scraped against the windshield and roof of my car.

As we drove along, slow but steady, the eyes of these alley-dwellers tracked our every move. Some with red-rimmed eyes, others with the wild, glassy-eyed look of people out of touch with reality. My palms grew moist.

It was difficult, looking at these people at their most

vulnerable, not wanting to stare and yet needing to look for her. For Genevieve.

I rode the brakes as people stood and encroached onto the road. Finally, I was forced to stop altogether when a thin, gangly man in ripped sweatpants and a food-stained sweater that read *Christian Soldier* stood directly in front of the car, eyes the colour of burnt toast.

We stared at one other.

"Oh, shit," Adriana muttered.

I took a deep breath. "Let me handle this. Stay in the car, okay?"

There must have been something about the look on my face that told her I was serious, because she nodded, her skin pasty, all the blood having left her face.

I got out of the car and shut the door behind me, tapping the window and pointing at the locks. Adriana nodded and locked the doors. Now I was alone, deep in the slums of Denver, facing a man who didn't look to be in his right mind at all.

"Who the hell are you?" the man growled as he made his way around to the side of the car. I didn't want to move any closer because of his stench. He smelled as if he lived inside a dumpster. I straightened my back and stepped toward him.

"I'm looking for my mother. She was last seen here," I said. We squared off, facing one another. He was a good six inches shorter than me, but looked crazy enough to still cause some damage.

"What's her name?" he asked.

"Genevieve."

The man's dirty face didn't move, but his eyes narrowed. "No one here by the name of Gen-of-eve."

"She may be known by a different name." I shifted my weight when he took another step closer. Now we were a mere foot or two apart, and the man's particular malodorous fragrance was enough to trigger my gag reflex. I swallowed it back. "I'll show you a picture."

He stood there without comment, waiting for me, his hostile expression firmly planted on his face. I dug the photo out of my back pocket and held it out to him.

Recognition flickered in the man's eyes. "This here ain't no Genevieve. This here is Jennie."

"So you know her?"

"Jennie don't live around here no more. Not after those people came and—" The man stopped, mid-sentence, his eyes suddenly widening, as if he were seeing me in a new light. "You ain't a Government man, are you?"

I shook his head. "No. I'm trying to find her, that's all."

The man backed up and I noticed his hands were shaking. What was he afraid of?

Then he yelled at the top of his lungs, "This man's here for Jennie! He wants to get our Jennie, just like the Government men!"

Like a slow-motion parody of a horror film the homeless descended on me like a pack of mangy, rabid coyotes that'd cornered a lone dog. They pressed up against me and pushed me back and forth, as if I was in a game of Red Rover with the most heinous smelling humans on earth.

"Kalan!" Adriana called out the window.

My head bobbed back and forth as I tried to maintain my cool. "Adriana, stay in the car!" I called out, but the car door slammed shut. Too late.

"Stop it!" Adriana yelled from the other side of the car. "He's looking for his mother! Stop it!"

The shoving ceased at once, but there were still a myriad of grubby hands grasping me with varying degrees of tightness. One person held me by the shoulder, fingers digging into my clavicle.

Adriana pushed her way closer, forcing the people aside. She was so brave.

"Your mama is Jennie?" asked one filthy, dirt-smeared woman.

"Yes, his mother is Jennie!" Adriana blurted out. "Now get your fucking hands off him!"

The group of ten or so of them stared back and forth between Adriana and me before turning to dumpster man for direction.

His face curled up into a snarl. "Bullshit! They're Government!"

The group instantly turned into a frenzy of screaming, fists flying and feet kicking. Pain blasted through my body from the various points of contact: knees, jaw and stomach. Adriana screamed amidst the sounds of angry voices.

I had to do something.

I dug deep into that dark part of me I kept locked up, the part that only Marcus had been witness to before this moment.

I pulled on it, and like an explosion, the fury ripped through my body and out, engorging my muscles and filling me with a burst of energy. One-by-one, I threw the people off of me as if they were tiny children. It wasn't until every last one of them was on the ground that I finally saw the shock in Adriana's expression as she looked at me, her mouth open.

My eyes were undoubtedly blood-red, haemorrhaged from the internal pressure. It had happened once before, when I was mugged. I looked away until the strange sensation inside me waned.

I surveyed those getting back up to their feet. Would they come back for another round? Their leader stayed on the ground, flat on his back while the others scattered away. I crouched down on my haunches by the man and grabbed him by the collar, lifting his head an inch off the ground.

"Where is Jennie? Tell me now."

He stared, his eyes watery, his gaze faraway. It was as if he wasn't even seeing me. I shook him a little, enough to jostle him out of his dissociative state.

"Please. I need to find my mother. Where is she?" The scent of rot emanated from every pore of the man's being.

He cringed. "She ain't been around here for at least six months."

I waited for him to continue, but he didn't. "Then where is she?"

The man began to laugh, his entire body vibrating beneath my grip. I tightened my hold on his shirt collar. The fabric was stiff in my hand.

He opened his eyes and peered up at me, the hostility rolling off of him in waves. "Maybe you should try the warehouse district."

The abandoned warehouse district was one of the most dangerous parts of Denver. Even more dangerous than it was here. My chest tightened at the thought of my mother living in such violence and squalor.

I let go of his collar slowly and lowered him back to the ground to prepare for the mind-meld. Then he made a sudden violent move upward, head-butting me in the forehead. Pain ricocheted around in my head, my nose erupted with a gush of blood and my skull throbbed. My knees almost buckled.

Adriana's scream rang out. "No!"

She kicked him square in the jaw, so hard he hit the ground beside me.

Despite the streaming blood from my nose and the throbbing in my head, I stood up. Adriana had a feral look on her face, all fierceness and anger in her curled lips and narrowed eyes. The man lay on his back holding his jaw. On further inspection, the grimace on his face and neck was a testament to the level of force Adriana put behind that kick.

I glanced around at all of the faces, staring at us. Watching.

"Let's get out of here," I said, grabbing Adriana's hand

We returned to the car and Adriana got in the driver's seat. We drove off, not a single person standing in our way.

*Did you know our genes represent only 2 per cent of the DNA in
our chromosomes? The other 98 per cent is non-coded DNA.
Scientists still don't know the purpose of this non-coding DNA.
-Your World, Biotechnology & You*

## CHAPTER EIGHT

### ADRIANA SINCLAIR

We were almost at the edge of the warehouse district. I
drove this time so Kalan could tend to his bloody nose and get in
and out of the car with ease, in the event of another incident like
the one in the back alley. It was my last chance to ask before we
arrived.

"Why did your eyes turn red back there?" I asked.

He looked down. "Pressure inside my head. It happens only
when I do something out of the ordinary. You know. Use my super
powers."

I laughed at his attempt at a joke, even though he looked
grim. "Does this happen often?"

"No. But remember, I've only started to accept and use
these abilities. Maybe it'll go away, or maybe it'll get worse. I don't
know."

"What about Marcus? Do his eyes do it?"

He contemplated for a moment. "Come to think of it, I've never seen it happen. But maybe that's because I have to try so hard. It comes easy to him."

Finally, an off-ramp led to the worst part of Denver. I pulled onto it.

"This is a bad idea," Kalan said. "I don't think we should go in there. What if he's setting us up? Telling us to go somewhere he knows we'll end up attacked?"

I scrutinized the weathered brick, the faded wood signs, the crumbled concrete walkways and the old buildings that seemed on the verge of collapse. Once again, people were scattered about in random places, sitting and leaning against signposts, lying on broken up segments of crushed cement, walking across barren landscape.

I parked Kalan's car on the side of the road, deserted of any other vehicles.

"We've come all this way and if we leave now, we'll have no more answers than we did yesterday," I said.

"Yeah, well, yesterday I didn't know my mother lived on skid row."

I set my hand on his arm. Sunlight caught his silvery eyes and exaggerated the high contrast of his pitch-black pupil. "We're here to find her. Let's do what we came for."

He smiled. His smile made me feel better. He might have strange, scary powers reminiscent of some kind of mutant superhero, but at his core I was certain Kalan was a good, decent man. "I know it's dangerous, but we made it through last time, didn't we? I'm sure we can get through it."

Kalan nodded. "We may not be so lucky this time."

"I need to know the truth. I need to understand the truth about me and my blood and why you and Marcus are the way you are. You heard the homeless guy. If we don't find out, we're probably going to have people come for us."

"If I believed they really were Government, I'd feel relieved."

"Who do you think they are?" I asked. "Scientists, like my grandmother and great-aunt believe?"

"I don't know." Kalan's expression was odd and unreadable as he cleared his throat. "Probably. Scientists with a very specific agenda."

I took a deep breath and let it out in a long puff. "We aren't going to figure this out without finding out more. It's time."

Kalan took in a long, deep breath. "Okay."

We got out, entwined our hands and set off across the road, toward a small group of people sitting in a semi-circle. As we approached them some turned toward us, others, away.

"Excuse me. We're looking for this woman," I said. I held the picture up.

Nobody responded. Kalan held out his hand for the photo and I gave it to him. He stepped over to a man in a denim jacket, his dark hair long and curly around his shoulders. Kalan lowered himself to one knee in front of the man. A murmur rippled through the group.

"This is my mother, Jennie. I'm trying to find her."

The man shook his head. "Sorry."

Kalan left him and approached a different man, a redhead sporting a worn out jean jacket, thick eye glasses and a bulbous, heavily veined nose. Big Red. "Have you seen her?"

The red-haired man reached out for the photo, his fingernails black with filth. He peered at it through the glasses and his mouth twitched at the corner. "I might have."

Kalan bit his lower lip. "I have cash. How much do you want?"

The guy nodded. "Two hundred. I want cigarettes, too. Camels. No filter."

"Done." Kalan took the photo back, stood up and came to me. "Off for cigarettes, I guess."

We returned to Kalan's car and drove to the nearest convenience store. It was located at the edge of the ghetto with thick steel bars covering the windows and doors. The clerk at the front had long hair pulled back into a tight ponytail, a tattooed teardrop under his left eye and tattoos across each knuckle. LOVE. HATE. There were cameras on the ceiling at all four corners of the store.

Kalan asked for the cigarettes at the checkout. The clerk

eyed him with beady eyes and pulled the smokes off a rack on the wall behind him and rang the price into the cash register without speaking a word to us. A few tense moments later we were back in the car, racing back to the red-haired man with our information.

When we got back to the same location where we'd left him and the rest of the people, they were gone.

"Fuck. What the hell?" Kalan muttered. Just then, a flash of movement caught the corner of my eye. I turned in time to see a baseball bat being waved at Kalan. It was the red-haired man and the others, all nearest Kalan on the driver's side of the car.

"Don't get out!" I said.

"I have to. They'll smash the windshield if I don't. Wait here. Please. Just... please wait." He got out before I could respond and shut the door behind him.

Kalan appeared calm and composed as he offered the bat-wielding Big Red the cigarettes. Then the guy said something to Kalan but I couldn't hear it. Kalan shook his head.

Big Red swung the baseball bat back behind his head, red hair flying. He pulled it down and to the side in one fell swoop. I screamed as Kalan ducked. I got out of the car just as Big Red staggered backward with the momentum of the bat, then steadied himself again. He turned sideways and crouched in a batting stance and started to swing again. Kalan launched himself at the guy in one long stride and the distance between them closed faster than my eye could track. Kalan grasped the bat mid-air, pulled it from him and shoved him backward. Big Red landed on the crushed concrete, skidding on his behind with his long hair flopped over his face, blocking the view of his expression. His groans said it all.

It all happened in the time it took me to get to Kalan's side of the car.

Big Red's friends shuffled backward away from Kalan. Away from me.

"Ready to talk?" Kalan asked, his breath heaving.

Big Red pushed his stringy red hair back from his face. A trickle of sweat squiggled down his temple. "I'll talk."

#

The Gold Strike was a long-abandoned hotel that had become something of a regular news feature in Denver, on account of the fact that it was a well-known residence of squatters, stabbings, overdoses and drug deals gone bad.

The front door was held closed with a nail and wire. Kalan unlatched it, and squeezed my hand. "Are you sure about this?"

"I'm sure."

We plunged into the darkness of the old lobby. After a few moments my eyes adjusted to the dimness.

The wooden front desk remained intact, but it had holes in the frame and was covered in graffiti. The floor appeared to be pale white marble but was hardly visible through the dirt, dust and grime smeared on top.

"Where are the people?" I whispered. Surely with this

much floor space, there would be a few people squatting down here?

"I don't know." Kalan tugged at my hand. "Let's go up?"

I nodded. To the left was a spiral staircase made of wrought iron and wood that snaked around to the second floor. The marble stairs were worn into a permanent u-shape.

The higher we climbed, the darker it got, with the only light coming through a few tiny windows near the landing of the second floor. With each step, more clutter tripped us. A shoe, used needles, charred aluminum foil. Food garbage was everywhere. The stench was unlike anything I'd smelled before, far worse even than the hoodlums in the back ally, and came from tin cans, milk jugs, vomit and piles of human excrement. My guts churned.

I stumbled—a stuffed toy? Kalan grabbed my elbow to keep me from falling directly on top of it, but not before I got a closer look. A dead cat. Bile backed up my throat at the sight of it.

"Ugh!" I squeaked.

"Come over on this side near the banister," Kalan said.

I stepped to the other side of the staircase where it appeared to have a more used path with less garbage.

"God, it stinks," I said. I trudged up, wary of touching the banister.

The emptiness of the vacant first floor was at complete odds with the shoulder-to-shoulder people of the second floor. I could barely see in the dim light, but what I did see chilled me to the core. Bone-thin, most of them, in varying states of illness and disease. The smell here only added a new element—the stench of urine and human decay.

The burgundy carpet that had once covered this floor was now deteriorated to the point where in some places it was a fine brown dust. Wood shone through at various bald patches and blue-coloured foam underlay was broken off into cotton-ball sized chunks. The fancy velvet brocade wallpaper was mostly peeled off, with only a small jagged strips remaining around the top where hands couldn't reach.

Directly in the middle of the room was charred wood and ashes, the remains of a fire. Ringing it were cheap sleeping bags in primary colours, domed tents, dolls and toys and numerous full garbage bags.

My skin crawled. Every lucid gaze fixed on me and Kalan. The whites of those eyes shone in the dimness, amplifying the filth of their skin and hair.

Could Kalan's mother be here?

A low hum of muttering and various movements began. Kalan must have taken this as a cue, because his voice, strong and sure, rang out.

"I'm looking for my mother. Her name is Genevieve. Some people may know her as Jennie."

Another rustle of movement and whispering, but nobody came forward. Kalan shifted his weight from foot to foot. I wanted to reach out and hold his hand, but I was so damn scared I could hardly move.

"Have any of you seen my mother, Genevieve?" Kalan remained calm and commanding, his body tall. He took a step further into the room. I glanced back at the staircase, my leg muscles twitching.

A woman with frizzy mouse-coloured hair, a pronounced hunchback and curved-in shoulders pushed herself to standing and shuffled forward. Kalan immediately walked toward her.

"Don't you come any closer," she said.

Kalan stopped, his entire body tensing. He put his hands up. "I'm not here to cause problems. I'm here to find my mother."

The woman's bowed-forward frame lowered slightly, as if the force of gravity was too much. "That's not what Genevieve said."

Kalan sucked in a noisy breath. "You know her?"

The woman stooped forward even more. "You are not welcome here. Genevieve doesn't want to see you."

Kalan's shoulders drooped about two inches, almost as if his helium-filled body had been punctured with a sharp needle.

"I don't think I've made myself clear. I want to speak to her. That's all."

The woman took a hobbling step backward when a tall man who'd been leaning against the wall raced to her side. He focused on Kalan, his lips pulled back in a snarl to reveal rotten and missing teeth. Kalan stopped and the woman straightened with her protector now at her side. "She said there would be a day when the white one or the dark one might come. She said this day would happen."

"We're her children," Kalan said. "Of course we would come to find our mother!"

She shook her head, the frizzy hair whirling about. Dust and dandruff floated up from the action, the particles lit up by the dim stream of light from a window overhead. Her henchman glowered. While the two of them in their various stages of poor health would not normally be cause for concern, the fact that we were surrounded by people made them a formidable force. I clasped my hands behind my back to hide their trembling and attempted to steady my breath.

"No. She doesn't want to see you. She never wants to see you. You're a freak of nature, and she wishes her botched abortion had been successful!"

Now Kalan's head tilted back, as if he'd taken a blow to the face.

The woman pointed a gnarled finger at Kalan. "Get out of here. You aren't welcome here."

"But I just—"

"Get him out!" The woman's shrill shriek cut straight through me, sheering off every last nerve.

A flurry of activity ensued, screams and shouts as the group charged Kalan. I yelled as they shoved him into the decrepit floor. A loud crack rang out as Kalan's body met wood. I lunged for him and clawed at those in the dog pile. My nails scratched and tore at any skin or fabric my fingers came into contact with.

Somebody grabbed me around the waist and ripped me backward, flailing and shrieking Kalan's name. I was dragged into the stairwell and shoved down the stairs. I grasped at the banister and caught an iron rung, but momentum twisted my arm and forced me to let go. My elbow tangled between rungs and pain sliced white-hot through my elbow and shoulder. My feet continued to travel down the stairs and wrenched my arm even further.

I screamed at my assailant. A middle-aged man with long brown hair and a thick gray beard looked down at me with a smile on his face. His eyes were red, glossy and hooded.

My trapped arm stopped the descent and I twisted to right myself. Despite the terrible pain, I gingerly removed my arm from the banister.

My attacker's face remained fixed with that same smug expression.

"Don't think you're going back in there, bitch."

I shot him my most withering glare. My mind whirled as I tried to think of a solution. A sudden concussion of sound reverberated through the floor beneath my feet. My bearded attacker spun around and ran back in.

My sleeve was torn, and blood spread out from a central point on the fabric like red food dye in white icing. With my good arm, I held my injured arm tight to my side and went back up the stairs.

I entered the second floor and shrieked.

The dog pile on top of Kalan looked like a swarm of maggots. They writhed, twisted and flipped about. Kalan was almost covered and the way the angry horde flopped and bumped, it was clear Kalan was no match for the sheer number of people.

I went for them once again and with a bloodcurdling battle-cry, I grabbed the backs of shirts and flung people aside as hard as I could. The larger, more robust men were under them, and through the flurry of limbs and heads, Kalan's face came into sharp focus.

One whole side of his head and face was covered in blood, like a complicated latticework of crimson swirls. A scream tore from my throat and I jumped on the back of a larger man and clawed at his cheeks, his eyes, his neck. He yelled and yanked me off by the hair so I tumbled to the floor.

I scrambled back to my feet. The man was already right back on top of the maggoty heap.

The pile of people flew off Kalan in a burst. Their bodies hurdled through the air as if each person was merely the weight of a kitten.

Kalan, bloodied and bruised but now back on his feet, looked down at the people he'd tossed off of himself. They surrounded him on the floor in a six foot perimeter. His eyes flashed blood-red.

#

I dabbed gently at the blood on Kalan's face. Somehow his cuts were miraculously already partly healed, including the purple bruises under one eye that were now a pale greenish-yellow. We'd checked into the first decent hotel we found and tended to our injuries. Luckily, the hotel suite was impeccably clean, considering the rate per night.

"How is it possible you're healing so fast? I mean, your cuts are almost gone, your bruises..." I wiped a smear of dried blood from his lips. "Even your black eye is almost gone."

Kalan blinked as he gazed into my eyes, watching my every move. "It's one of the effects of my genetics. Rapid healing has been the one thing I've always appreciated about being different. I've been able to heal like this for as long as I can remember."

Here, in the bathroom light, Kalan's eyes were glossy and near colourless, like polished silver, the blood-red gone. I wanted so badly to lean down and kiss his silvery lashes that curled against his cheek. Instead, I made another slow stroke with the cloth to the side of his jaw, where blood had dried and stuck to his pale stubble. "I thought they were going to kill you."

Kalan touched my cheek. "I thought so too. When I saw him drag you to the stairwell... I almost went out of my mind. If they hadn't been tackling me at that moment, I would have torn him in half." He looked at me with intensity, a kind of deep intimacy I'd never experienced before with another human being.

A strange tightening sensation started in my belly and I set the washcloth back into the rusty-orange colored water in the sink. I evaluated his appearance, satisfied that most of the blood was cleaned off. He hadn't flinched once, not even when I'd scrubbed at his sore eye.

"The first time I saw you I thought you looked like an angel. Then, I thought you looked like a cartoon, some kind of angelic Superman. But now I realize you're not an angel or a superhero."

Kalan snorted. "No. I'm not."

"You're just a person. You may have chromosomal mutations and genetic abnormalities, but you and I are the same." I gathered his hands in mine. "We're human."

He looked into my eyes, blinking, but not saying a word.

"And it's because of our ordinary, average humanity that we're so much alike. We're flawed, we're weak, we have issues and family hang-ups. But doesn't it seem like when we're together, all of that is more easily endured? Like the flaws are smoother, the feelings softer around the edges, the hang-ups more tolerable?"

Kalan shook his head, his eyes closed. "I don't know why you're saying this. But I want to believe it. I need to believe it."

"What do you mean you don't know why I'm saying this?" I

asked. "You think I'm saying it to make you feel good about yourself?"

"I don't know. Nobody has ever said anything like that to me before." Kalan's voice was soft and low. "All I know is that I am... I think, I've—Oh, Jesus, Adriana."

I set my palm on his soft cheek and gazed into his eyes. The heat between us was almost palpable as he waited for my response. I let my hand drop away from his cheek. "What would have happened to us at the hotel, if you weren't so strong?" I asked.

Kalan's shoulders sagged a bit, obviously not expecting my question. He followed my every move, even as I pulled the plug in the sink and let out the bloody water.

"I don't know." His voice was quiet. "What would I have done if you'd been seriously injured? I would have gone out of my mind."

"Why? Why would you have been so shaken?" I swallowed, the memory of that moment with Derek, the day Analiese died, flooding me, washing away this temporary happiness. "I don't think you see me clearly," I said, washing blood from my hands. "You seem to think I'm better than I am."

His eyebrow crooked. "What is that supposed to mean?"

I felt like a bomb, ready to explode. I couldn't have him looking at me the way he did... He had to know the truth.

"I almost made out with my sister's boyfriend the day she died." I gasped from my abrupt admission and backed into the wall. It felt like every last ounce of oxygen had been stripped from my lungs. I imagined what he was thinking, *Wow, you are quite the colossal bitch-slut. I'm going to get up and leave now.*

Kalan peered at me, his expression impassive. "You said almost. What stopped you?"

My mouth twitched and my chin quivered. "I couldn't do it. I couldn't mess around with him."

"Why not?"

A salty tear burned its way down my raw cheek. "It was wrong."

"Did you want to?" Kalan asked.

A sob tore from my mouth. "Yes! I wanted him first, and do you know what she did after I told her? She fucked him! That same night. She seduced the one guy I liked and she never even apologized for it." Tears flowed from my eyes now, dripping from my chin to my chest. I glanced at the door.

Kalan caught where I was looking and stood up, grasping both of my hands. "Did she do it to hurt you?"

"Yes."

Kalan's thumbs stroked my palms. "Why?"

I bit my lip as another fresh round of sobs threatened at my throat. Finally, the words tore from my mouth, "Because I still had my innocence. And she could never get hers back."

Kalan pulled me into his arms, my chest heaving. He smelled like blood and sweat and Kalan. "She was in pain. Her world, her life, everything was unjust."

I pressed my cheek to his clavicle and breathed deeply. His supple skin was smooth beneath my lips. "I should have known that and understood it. But I didn't. Instead, I was angry. Hurt. I wanted to get her back."

"Of course you did. Who wouldn't?" Kalan's question was more of a statement.

"Anyone with half the emotional conscience of a gnat would have forgiven her, Kalan. But not me. Not Adriana. No, I had to hold onto the resentment, and wait until my opportunity came... and then..."

Kalan placed a finger under my chin and raised my head so my gaze met his. "You didn't do it. You'd forgiven her."

I closed my eyes, wishing so much his words were true. But the facts were the facts. I shook my head. "No. You don't understand."

"I think I do. I don't think *you* understand," Kalan said. His voice was firm but gentle.

"That's where you're wrong—"

"Forgiveness doesn't mean acceptance," he interrupted, "There's a difference. You understood, you forgave her, but that didn't mean you accepted what she did was okay. It wasn't okay. She hurt you. Betrayed you. And you had a right to be hurt and angry. But you still forgave her for it."

I gazed into silvery eyes that held mine, challenging me to

disagree. Was he right? I swiped the tears off of my face and turned away, pushing him off to the side. I set my hands on the sink and looked at my blotchy face in the mirror. I was such a train wreck. *Look at you. Alone in the world. Analiese gone forever. This is what you deserve.*

"I don't want to talk about this anymore," I said. Then I ran a clean cloth under some cold water and washed my face. The coolness soothed my chapped skin.

"You're not ready to stop punishing yourself yet?" Kalan asked.

I didn't respond. Instead, I took off my dirty shirt and threw it in the tub. "This is filthy. So are your pants."

Kalan looked down at himself and stripped down to his black boxers and sat down on the toilet seat. After having been under the dog-pile of dirty, sick, homeless people there wasn't a single item of outerwear that wasn't soiled.

I didn't want to stare at him, but it was hard not to look. I glanced away and touched my sore shoulder. It was warm under my fingertips.

"Does it hurt?" Kalan asked.

"Yes. But at least it isn't dislocated. Maybe just sprained? I'm pretty lucky all that's wrong is a tender shoulder and a bruise on my hip and elbow. Things would have been different if you'd just been a regular person." I tried to keep my eyes on his face and not look down at his body. I failed miserably.

Kalan smiled and his face lit up. Without clothing on, and despite the blood and bruises, he looked like a meticulously sculpted god, his skin pale and flawless as marble. The toned muscle of his body almost stood out more because of his paleness, the way the hills cast shadows on the valleys, his shoulders wide and round, his arms thick and defined. Just like the statue of David, I could look at him for hours.

I touched his swollen cheekbone. "Does this still hurt?"

His pupils dilated wide and black. "Not anymore." He placed his hands on either side of my hips and pulled me slowly toward him. When our bodies connected, he leaned in to me, wrapped his arms around my waist and rested his head on my stomach. I stroked his silken hair and wondered if he could feel the pounding of my heartbeat, matching his.

We'd been to hell and back.

"What do you think will happen when we really find out the truth?" I asked.

Kalan traced a line from my hipbone to my ribs, almost absently. "I think we'll need a lot of therapy."

"Funny."

Kalan shrugged. "I have no clue."

"Then I want to tell you something," I said. "If both of us are potentially going to need years of psychotherapy to deal with the truth of our existence, then I want you to know how I feel."

What was I going to say?

Kalan's eyes widened. They were so bright they looked like twin diamonds. "How do you feel?"

"I... I want—"

My words were cut off when Kalan pulled my face down and brushed his lips against mine. I wrapped my arms around his neck as he pulled me onto his lap. Our kisses were soft and gentle at first, but soon grew sharp with desperation and heat and... fear. His breathing staggered. Was it pain or the effort of restraint? His hunger was clear in the pressure of his lips, warring with his incredible effort to maintain control. His mouth was hot on mine, and he tasted like coppery blood. Was his mouth bleeding?

He tried to move with gentleness, but his movements were far from careful as he grasped the fabric of my camisole and tugged the hem up and over my head. His hands fisted my hair, winding through the strands so tight it almost hurt. The loss of control I felt was overwhelming. I gasped as my teeth came down on his lip, grazing it slightly. He moaned, a sound edged with both pain and pleasure.

I leaned against him, his pale skin warm against mine. I gazed at the curve of his collarbone, the swell of his shoulders, the dip between his hipbone and waist. So perfect. My fingers traced a line from his navel down to the waistband of his boxers. Kalan's entire body stilled, and his breath hitched in his throat as I ran my fingers over the skin of his hard stomach, just above his waistband. My heart pounded so hard, I wondered if he could hear it.

He kissed my throat, his breath hot against my clavicle. Each kiss was like an electric jolt straight from my neck right down to my toes. I shivered at the delicious intensity of the sensation. The intimacy.

"Adriana. If you want to stop, we can...?" His voice buzzed against the skin at my throat, sending more electrical shocks through my body.

"No."

"Are you sure?" Kalan asked.

"Yes. Are you?"

Our lips met again. His mouth was superheated now, impatient. Kalan groaned as my body melded against his chest. The image of Analiese, pressed against Derek flashed through my mind, but somehow, because of this moment of passion, the memory of that moment lost its usual emotional intensity.

"I've wanted this since the moment I met you." Kalan's voice was husky. "I've dreamed of this moment every day since then. You are what I've been waiting my whole life for."

Tears built at the back of my eyes, creating pressure and heat. "I have too," I whispered.

Then he smiled and kissed me with such ferocity I forgot to breathe. I moaned as pleasure rippled through me, jolts of heat straight to my core as fumbling fingers found the clasp of my black lacy bra.

Kalan dropped his gaze and looked me over with that

unbearable reverence once again. But this time, I revelled in it. "God. Look at you. You're beautiful," he said.

A quiver of excitement slid through me and I couldn't help but smile. I didn't deserve to be this happy, did I? The burning heat inside me ignited into a full-fledged blaze. Our tongues twined together, a slow erotic dance. Then I noticed his lips were swollen.

"Your mouth. It looks... sore. What's wrong?" I asked.

He licked his lips and smiled sheepishly. "I guess it's not only your tears that cause my skin to tingle."

I examined his lips, the way they were slightly redder than they usually were. My cheeks burned. "What?"

"You're like a superheating lubrication. But I've noticed it seems to be lessening. Maybe with exposure... maybe I'm building immunity to it."

I stared at Kalan. He smiled as if unperturbed while I felt like crawling under a rock.

"You make it sound like this is no big deal!" I turned to leave, but he stood up and grabbed my wrists, holding me in place with a gentle but firm grip.

"It's not a big deal. Just another genetic thing, I'm sure of it. Besides, it feels good," Kalan said, doing his best to put me at ease.

"Kalan, I... I can't." I left the bathroom.

*(There is) strong evidence that evil behavior—mass murder, armed robbery... might be caused by the right set of genes interacting with the wrong environment.*
*-Scientific American*

## CHAPTER NINE

### KALAN KANE

"I never want to get out of this bed," Adriana said from across the room.

My back ached from sleeping on the fold-out sofa bed and my feet hung off the end.

"I wish I could say the same."

Three loud raps at the hotel door rang out.

"Who would that be?" Adriana whispered.

I jumped out of bed, threw on my jeans and went to the door. Adriana disappeared into the bathroom to get dressed. I looked through the peephole.

The door blasted in and slammed into my shoulder so hard it propelled me backward against the wall. My neck wrenched from the impact.

"What the hell—"

"Hello, brother." Marcus stepped into the room. He wore

jeans, a black leather jacket and protective eyewear. His eyes glittered, his mouth curled up in a smug half-smile. Tait stood right behind him with a blank expression. Was he under Marcus's control? "Sorry about the door."

"What the...? Why are you here, Marcus?" I asked. My shoulder still ached from where the door rammed into me.

Marcus chuckled and walked in. He glanced at the bed, the rumpled sheets. "I got tired of waiting, and I saw a text on Tait's phone that you and Adriana were here looking for our mother behind my back."

The bathroom door opened. Adriana came out, her eyes narrowed, her mouth a hard, thin line.

"It wasn't behind your back," I started, "We found something—"

"Yes, yes. You found the picture at Uncle Les the Molester's house." Marcus smiled and his white teeth gleamed. "I already know this."

Adriana surveyed Tait. "Hey. Tait? Are you okay?" His vacant eyes spoke volumes. She reached out and snapped her fingers in front of his face. "Tait?"

Tait's eyebrows rose high on his forehead and he blinked. "What? I'm fine."

"Where is Zoe?" I asked.

Tait looked at Marcus, who gave him a barely perceptible nod. "At home. Where else would she be?" Tait said.

Marcus didn't give either of us time to respond to Tait. "The point is, you and Adriana went to find our mother without me," Marcus's nostrils flared. "That was not part of our agreement, Kalan."

"I didn't think it was a big deal," I said. "Obviously, I misjudged."

"Obviously," Marcus sneered.

Adriana glared at Marcus. "Is he under your control?" She gestured to Tait.

"Perhaps," Marcus said with a wave of his hand. "Now, I'd like a quick run-through of everything you've discovered so far. No more secrets. No more skulking around behind my back."

"It wasn't like that," I said.

Without warning, Marcus grabbed my throat and squeezed. My throat closed in on itself and my whole body convulsed. I grasped at Marcus's fingers to pry them off as a gurgling noise erupted from my mouth.

Adriana shrieked. "Stop it Marcus!"

Marcus let go and the relief was instantaneous. I leaned forward and gasped for breath. *Fuck.* Why had I allowed myself to trust him when every gut instinct inside of me had screamed to stay the hell away from him? Brother or not, he was nearly a stranger to me, barely more than someone off the street. Hell, I knew the street hobo about as well as I knew Marcus.

And now Adriana had seen me completely emasculated by

my own brother.

"What the hell did you do that for?" Adriana demanded.

"Why don't you ask Kalan?" Marcus's brow arched, his mouth quirked on one side. "Brother, why did I do that to you?"

My voice came out in a rasp. "He's angry we went to find our mother without him."

Adriana's eyes widened and she spoke through gritted teeth. "You won't get anything out of us if you continue to hurt Kalan."

Marcus laughed. "Oh, I think you're incorrect on that point." His stance changed, ever-so-slightly, and then with lightning speed he had his hand wrapped around Adriana's neck. Her eyes saucered and her mouth flopped open with a gurgle.

She wrenched sideways and managed to sink her teeth into his fist. He jerked his hand back involuntarily but then it was back around her throat the next instant.

"Hmm. Your nasty spit burns my skin, isn't that interesting? Luckily, it's not bad enough to stop me." Marcus practically snarled into her face.

"Stop!" I leaped over to Adriana. "Stop! I'll tell you anything you want to hear!"

Marcus let her go. She sucked in rough, gasping breaths.

"Thank you. It's so much easier if you'd all just cooperate," Marcus said, stretching his hands out and cracking his knuckles. Adriana's chest continued to heave, her eyes glassy.

I had no choice.

I told him everything, from the street brawl to the attack in the abandoned hotel. Marcus listened intently during the entire explanation.

"Back to the hotel," Marcus said. "Where you failed, brother, I will succeed."

#

This time, when we entered the lobby of the abandoned hotel, the stench was even worse than before. Something had obviously died in there, and not only was it decomposing but was beginning to putrefy. I swallowed back on the gag reflex and put my hand over my mouth, which did nothing to mask the smell anyway. *This is my personal version of hell.* Stink, human misery, humiliation at the hands of my brother, and the girl I was falling for witnessing it all.

Marcus appeared indifferent to the odour. His eyes glittered black like polished coal with a hard, determined look that made my skin crawl. Adriana's lips were pressed together. I grasped her hand.

Tait followed along, directly behind Marcus, as if he were tied to him by some invisible tether, never straying more than a few feet. And while he looked like himself, his hollow responses and oddly blank expressions told me he was far from normal.

Now the wooden check-in desk had a giant hole kicked in the front on the left side so the heavy marble top slanted in the start of a collapse. Marcus took the stairs two at a time. Unfazed by the darkness as we climbed higher, he lithely sidestepped the litter and debris on the floor. He didn't even notice the dead cat, which now looked far more flat than it had the day before.

Once we reached the landing of the second floor, my mind flashed back to the attack that had taken place less than twenty-four hours prior. Perspiration broke out under my collar.

Marcus went in first. A hush fell over the room, every person waiting, watching Marcus as if he was a preacher preparing to deliver a sermon of Hell and brimstone.

Marcus's baritone voice rang out in the decrepit room. "Genevieve. Your sons are here to see you."

A voice responded from within the depths of the room. "Nobody here by that name."

"Genevieve. You will respond or your friends will pay," Marcus said. "You know this is true."

The silence that ensued made my nerves sing. People glanced back and forth from one another, but in the dimness, their expressions were unreadable.

There was a choking sound. Who was Marcus choking? I cringed at the remembrance of the pain, the complete and utter sense of panic at being unable to breathe. Then a commotion broke out and several people stood up and staggered about, their hands around their necks. Their eyes bulged from their red faces.

"What—?" I turned to Marcus. "How are you doing this?"

He smiled at me. "I've got lots of tricks you don't know

about. Wait and see."

I watched in helplessness as choking sounds continued and faces turned to shades of purple and blue. Was Marcus using telekinesis? If he was, we were in far more danger than I'd even realized. Marcus was actually unstoppable. This was beyond bad.

"Marcus," I whispered, "Stop."

Marcus ignored me and maintained his focus on the group. The gagging and choking continued and several of the people dropped to their knees, others fell flat on the floor. The sounds combined into a single, high-pitched wheezing.

Adriana shrieked. "Please. Stop! You're hurting them."

A woman stumbled forward, her arm raised and waving. She came directly at Marcus, her brilliant teal eyes flashing.

"Marcus," I grabbed his arm. "It's her."

All at once, the woman and the rest of the people took a deep, gasping breath. The teal-eyed woman fell to her knees on the deteriorating floor. She had exactly the same shape of eyes as me and Marcus, deep-set with long black lashes. But where my eye colour was silver and Marcus's were black, hers were the same vivid teal as Adriana's.

Marcus took a menacing step toward her, the tips of his shoes at her side. She peered at him from inside a blue hooded sweater, her face dark, as if she hadn't washed in days, her skin ruddy and thick.

She stood up, her gaze fixed on Marcus. "I'm Genevieve."

I approached her, my legs rubbery, my mind and body somehow at war with one another. This was undeniably my biological mother. I stared into eyes that were so familiar, and yet, I'd never seen them before in my entire life. As I approached her, those eyes grew wider and wider, until she shut them altogether. She held her hand up in a Stop! gesture.

I came to an abrupt halt, my mouth dry as sandpaper. Marcus eyed her with lips pulled back in contempt.

Genevieve's eyes opened. "Don't come any closer."

I nodded slowly. "Okay."

"What, mother?" Marcus said, his voice mocking. "No hugs and kisses for your long lost boys? No bittersweet reunion that could be a made-for-TV movie? Or, better yet, a reality show?"

Genevieve's gaze flicked back and forth from Marcus to me, and I could almost see the wheels turning inside her head. Undoubtedly, she was evaluating who was the most dangerous of the two of us.

"No, Marcus. I'm afraid not," Genevieve said. She spoke to him with confidence, no hint of fear.

Marcus's expression changed slightly. "You know our names. That's a surprise. I expected you to have given us the titles of Scary Baby One and Scary Baby Two."

Now there was no denying the bitterness in Marcus's voice, belying the cool, arrogant expression. Were his angry words only a veneer? Years of varnish coated over the sadness and pain of rejection and abandonment?

In contrast, Genevieve's expression was obvious. Her eyes were wide and flashing, her mouth down at the corners.

"I named you, Marcus. But I couldn't keep you. For everyone's safety."

Marcus stared at her, his black eyes hard as coal. "Is that so, Mom?"

Genevieve grimaced. The word mom dripped with sarcasm, the sting of it biting. She took a quick glance back at the hoard of people who watched the spectacle, obviously too afraid to intervene on her behalf.

She addressed both me and Marcus. "Let's talk in private."

Marcus made no attempt to move, but when she stepped by him, he grabbed her by the shoulder and brought her to an abrupt halt. He leaned in to her ear, but spoke loud enough for all of us to hear. "Don't pull any stunts. Got it?"

Genevieve looked him straight in the eye, but didn't respond. She shrugged his hand off of her arm and continued walking away. Marcus let her go and followed her descent down the spiral staircase with Tait faithfully at his heels. I glanced at Adriana and reached for her hand. Clutching one other, we set off behind them.

In the lobby at the bottom she slowed and spoke to Marcus. "I go no further."

Marcus stopped, Tait beside him. He laced his fingers through Tait's, who smiled in response. Adriana and I exchanged glances.

"You're so wrong, mother," Marcus's head was tilted to the side as if he was goading her. "You're coming with me. With us, actually. Oh, and I almost forgot to mention the most important part." He looked directly at me, his cheek twitching, as if stifling a laugh. "We're all going to meet dad."

Genevieve shrieked.

"What?" I felt like I'd been struck by a bus. "What did you just say?"

"It is the best part, isn't it?" Marcus chuckled. "Kalan, you're not the only one doing things behind people's backs. As it turns out, I've had a little secret of my own, all this time. I was almost feeling guilty about it, early on when we decided to pair up and work together to find mom, but after the stunt you and Adriana pulled... well, I don't feel much guilt anymore. You really can't trust people. Thanks for reminding me of that."

"No! No, you can't do that," Genevieve was nearly crying. "He'll do things... to all of us." Her face was white beneath the layers of grime. "Like he did to me when he worked at the Center for Inherited Disease Research."

Adriana's eyes flashed with recognition.

"Marcus, I—"

He cut me off. "Shhh. None of you want a sore throat, do

you?" He didn't wait for a reply, but instead grasped Genevieve around the bicep and pulled her to the car. Tait reluctantly let go of his hand.

Marcus insisted Genevieve sit in the front passenger seat, and Adriana, Tait and me in the back. With her in the car, it smelled like a stale, wet sock. From my vantage point, her hair appeared to not have been combed for days, or perhaps even weeks. The near-black strands had an undercoat of grease near the roots, the ends matted into snarled swirls.

How in the world could this be my mother? How could she survive this lifestyle? What could possibly happen to lead a person to live this kind of life?

What was Marcus up to? How had he learned of our father, but I hadn't? Had our father reached out to him, or did Marcus find him? There were so many questions I wanted to ask, but I no longer trusted Marcus to tell me the truth like he no longer trusted me. It had become a surreal nightmare, fed by the energy of his anger. Not by choice, I was about to meet my father after meeting my mother the very same day. I'd spent my whole life dreaming of that kind of moment, all of those fantasies a varied version of the same theme—hugs, smiles and apologies for giving me up. Yet the way that this meeting was taking place couldn't have been more different from what I'd imagined.

Our mother sat up tall and dignified in her seat, her back ramrod straight. Despite the ruddy appearance of her skin, she didn't look emaciated and unhealthy the way some of the others in the hotel had. However, her clothing was scraggly and dishevelled, her windbreaker-style jacket dirty and stained where it covered numerous other layers.

I couldn't wait to ask questions. I had to know things. Even though it was under the worst possible conditions, with Marcus dictating the situation, I'd waited my entire life to talk to her and I didn't know if I'd get another chance. "Genevieve, are you related to Virginia..." I turned to Adriana for help.

"Virginia MacLean," Adriana said.

Genevieve bristled at the mention of the name. "Is she still alive?"

"No," Adriana said. "She passed away. Two weeks before Marcus and Kalan were born."

Even though Genevieve's expression didn't change, I saw her chest heave and her eyes water. "Virginia deserved better than that."

"Mother," I said, finding the term odd and out of place. "How is it that you and Virginia looked so similar? We were told you were nearly identical, despite being several years apart in age and having no known relatives in common."

She gave Marcus a sidelong glance. "This situation is precisely what I wanted never to happen. The two of you and me together. And to think there are more of us. More women with this cursed DNA." She spoke directly to Adriana, her voice rising. "But it has happened. All those years of keeping secrets, hiding, all for nothing. Marcus, you don't know what you have put in motion here!" Marcus glanced at her outburst but didn't respond. Genevieve turned to me after a moment of slow breaths. "Kalan, let me ask you, how old were you when you realized you had a twin?"

"I was six."

"Is that the first time you knew?" she asked. "I'm not talking about the first time you and Marcus met, I'm asking you about the first time you knew you had a twin."

I shrugged. "I guess I've always known." A muscle in Marcus's neck twitched.

"That's right," Genevieve said. "And let me ask you this. Is there any other way for there to be two people on this planet, who are not twins, but who have the exact same DNA?"

I suddenly knew exactly what she was getting at. "Are you a clone of Virginia?"

"I am."

Her admission, quietly stated, made my ears ring. Adriana squirmed and her mouth dropped open. Even Marcus turned back and gaped.

Our mother was a clone. Of Adriana's what? second cousin? We were... related.

Adriana folded over in her seat, her head in her hands. My heart felt like it had shrunk, withered with a complete loss of potential. We were related. Could we even be together? I placed my hand on her now quaking back. Would there ever be an end to these miserable discoveries for her? How many more wretched things were going to happen before Adriana's psyche broke under the pressure?

"Where are you taking us?" Genevieve asked, breaking the silence. Her voice had a familiar tenor, a vocal quality both me and Marcus shared. "To Malcolm's lab?"

Marcus glanced at her, his eyes narrowed. "That's not up for discussion."

"How well do you know him, Marcus? I'm venturing a guess that you know very little about what he is capable of." Genevieve wrung her hands in her lap.

"Malcolm. Is that the name of our father?" I asked.

Genevieve nodded as she looked out the car window at the terrain whipping by. "Yes. What you need to know right now is about his ambition. This is a man who is singularly focused on achievement, personal gain, at the expense of anyone around him."

Marcus sneered. "He's a scientist. They're all like that."

"No, Marcus. They're not all like Malcolm." Her hands suddenly stilled. "Malcolm's father was an alcoholic. He was an educated man, a geneticist, with a side interest in cross-breeding animals. He had his own hobby ranch where he raised many... odd species." She paused, her expression slightly disgusted, as if remembering something particularly reprehensible from that ranch.

"His father, Gordon, was far more interested in his creatures and his booze than he was in your father. He spent thousands of hours away from home, in the lab and in the field, for the sake of his own vanity. Recognition and prestige from the scientific community was more important to him than a bond with his son. His need to manipulate genetics in new and unique ways fuelled the narcissism within him. I don't know if the alcohol was the catalyst that made him so thoughtless and reprehensible or if it was his true personality. Malcolm was a straight-A student, on the honor roll every year, played the violin and graduated a year ahead of schedule, but his father never thought he was good enough. If Malcolm got an A-minus, his father would mock him for not getting an A-plus. He continually reminded Malcolm that he had graduated two years ahead, rendering Malcolm's one year insignificant. Malcolm said he never stopped trying to impress him, and almost every educational and career choice Malcolm made was to please his father. But Malcolm was seeking something that he would never find. His father was incapable of giving Malcolm what he wanted: approval. Gordon's alcohol dependency worsened every year, until finally, when Malcolm was preparing to defend his Ph.D. dissertation in gene sequencing, his father fell ill. Cirrhosis of the liver. Malcolm went to his death bed, hoping his father would finally give him what he'd sought from him his whole life. Malcolm thought that surely when a person was facing death they would take a moment to reflect upon and appreciate the accomplishments of his only son. He went to him, minutes before his last breath, and asked his father if he'd made him proud. Do you know what Gordon said?"

The entire car was silent. "What did he say?" I asked.

"He said there was only one thing that Malcolm could do to impress him. And that was to engineer a genetically superior human." Genevieve's voice grew thick. Did she have feelings for our father? "But we all know there is no such thing. Gordon laughed in his son's face and said, 'But that will never happen, will it, Malcolm? Not by you, anyway.'" She cleared her throat. "I think that was the day everything good inside of him shattered. All hope, all sensitivity for others, gone with that single, thoughtless sentence from a dying, selfish old man."

Adriana kicked at Marcus's seat. "Look what you've done. You're taking us to him."

"Shut up!" Marcus yelled.

"Wait," Adriana said. "Who cloned you in the first place?"

Genevieve pursed her lips and gave Adriana a sad smile. "Remember how I told you about Gordon's interest in cross-breeding? He also enjoyed genetic sequencing. Like father, like son."

My grandfather had cloned my biological mother. Then my father had impregnated her. I was related to Adriana, the girl I'd just almost had sex with. My twin brother betrayed me. My reality spun, a million miles an hour. A hell-storm in my head.

My fists clenched and I shoved Marcus's seat from behind. It hit the back of Marcus's head. "Why are you doing this?" I said through gritted teeth.

Marcus slammed hard on the brakes, and even from the back I could see his jaw flex. *Here we go.* Marcus and I jumped out of the car. The attack was sudden, my entire right side compressed as I hit the asphalt. Marcus's fist connected with my temple and sent shooting pains throughout my entire skull. My teeth rattled.

The car doors opened and Adriana yelled while I fought through waves of blurred vision and nausea.

Then a voice rang out, crystal-clear and familiar, although I'd only heard it for the first time moments ago. My mother's voice. Except... I didn't hear it with my ears. Her voice was inside my head.

*"Kalan. Surrender to him. You can't defeat him right now, and he's willing to kill you if you don't. You're more powerful than him, I know you are. But you don't know your strengths yet, do you?"*

Marcus's shoe made contact with my ribs with a wet crack. Jolts of white-hot fire burned through my torso. Adriana screamed, and from the dark corner of my eye, I saw her jump on Marcus's back.

The world tipped on its side and everything went black.

#

When I awoke, the pain had dissipated. I was in pitch darkness. I bounced and lurched back and forth on my side. The trunk? It had to be. There was still a chemical new-car smell that itched in my throat.

Within moments, the car rolled to a stop and the engine turned off. A beat later, sunlight assaulted my senses as the trunk opened and Marcus reached in to grasp my arm and yank me out. I toppled out of the car and fell on my knees, stones biting into my kneecaps. I ignored the pain and forced myself to my feet. Adriana cried out as she rushed around the side of the car, her eyes wide as she wrapped her arms protectively around me.

Marcus flashed us a mocking smile. "Bumpy ride?"

I didn't give him the satisfaction of a response. Instead, I focused my attention on Adriana. "Are you okay? Did he do anything to you?"

She shook her head as tears streamed down her face. "No. I'm fine. But I thought... I didn't know if you were okay, and—" Her voice pinched off in her throat. I held her tight while Marcus watched, his lip curved upward.

Genevieve got out of the car, her eyes blazing.

Had she spoken to me telepathically? Or did I imagine it?

With the way she studied us right now, suspicion obvious in her narrowed, watchful gaze, I couldn't be sure.

I glanced around. We were parked in front of a massive silver and grey building with reflective windows that gave the whole edifice the appearance of a twelve story-high mirror. The sign on the outside of the building said EROS.

"Where are we?" I asked.

Marcus smirked. "We're at Daddy's place."

*Genomic research began with the Human Genome Project (HGP), the international research effort that determined the DNA sequence of the entire reference human genome, completed in April 2003.*
*-National Human Genome Research Institute*

## CHAPTER TEN

### KALAN KANE

I pulled Adriana as close to me as humanly possible. Marcus began to stride towards the atrium of the massive corporate structure. None of the rest of us moved. Marcus stopped and wheeled about, eyes flashing with the same intense look I had seen at the abandoned hotel, hand raised. With his other hand, he motioned for us to follow. For a heartbeat we stood, resisting him. Then slowly, Genevieve began to move to follow. Adriana briefly looked up at me and then moved to follow suit, her hand pulling mine along. I allowed her to lead me across the flagstone walkway and into the atrium.

The inside of the building mimicked the exterior, with the lobby area vaulted all the way up. Floor-to-ceiling windows made the interior as bright as broad daylight. Each floor was visible, the walkways glassed-in. People moved about on the various floors in their white lab coats, scurrying in and out of hallways and rooms like scuttling insects.

A woman at a reception desk was the first to see us, and a glimmer of unidentifiable emotion passed over her face, right before she composed herself and flashed a gracious smile.

"Hello and welcome to Eros. Dr. Bellamy is waiting for you."

I swallowed. Dr. Malcolm Bellamy. My father.

The woman pressed a button on her headset as her fingers rapidly tapped a telephone keypad. "Dr. Bellamy's visitors have arrived."

Not even two seconds later, four security guards strode up. Their uniforms were gunmetal gray and shrouded in bulletproof body armour and a gun belt festooned with ammunition, a club, a radio and a handgun, the most obvious and terrifying piece of equipment out of them all.

I shivered. Adriana stared at the formidable men, as did Marcus, who observed their approach with smug satisfaction. Beyond Marcus was my mother, who's flashing eyes and shallow breaths clearly displayed exactly how she was feeling.

One guard with deeply etched crows-feet around his eyes and a heavy uni-brow spoke to us in a monotone, mechanical voice. "This way."

Marcus gestured to follow, with a glib wave of his hand. I wanted nothing more than to punch him on the side of the head. Instead, I mouthed the words *fuck you* to him. Marcus smiled and winked.

The guards surrounded us in the elevator, even keeping Marcus at arm's length. The elevator whizzed up to the fifth floor where we were prodded to exit. The security team escorted us down a long, brightly lit corridor with various labs on either side. Finally, we came to the double doors of a large corner office.

We filed in, one by one, the guards watching our every move. A man sat behind a massive wooden computer desk. He had grey hair and a freckled, pale complexion. He smiled. His two front teeth had a huge gap between them.

"Welcome! Genevieve, it's so nice to see you again. I trust my staff have kept you feeling safe here?" His voice was soft and gentle, his English accent highly pronounced.

Genevieve responded immediately. "Malcolm. I should have known you would find us eventually. There are no limits to the lengths you will go to achieve your goal, is there?"

"Genevieve. I am so sorry to learn you have lived a life of suffering." Malcolm stood to greet us. He was tall and fit for his age, his body morphology similar to Marcus and me. He stopped directly in front of Genevieve.

She held Malcolm's gaze with a steely expression. "I've contemplated suicide over the years, but I was afraid you would have dug me up and used my corpse for genetic material."

This elicited a burst of laughter from Malcolm, his laugh quiet but choppy and staggered, almost like a coughing fit. "You know me all too well."

He placed a hand on Marcus's shoulder. "Well done, Marcus. Well done, indeed."

"Thank you," Marcus said.

Malcolm continued to survey each and every one of us. He looked Tait over from head to toe but didn't acknowledge him. Then he approached me and Adriana. "This must be Kalan and Adriana. I am so delighted to finally meet the two of you. You are both exactly what I expected, although Kalan, you are much more handsome than I expected."

"What do you want with us?" I asked.

Malcolm peered into my eyes, as if examining their strange silver quality. He stepped back and responded, "You'll find out soon enough. Please, do have some patience with this process, for I have had to patiently wait for you." My hands fisted.

Then he spoke to Adriana. "Miss Sinclair. Fabulous. Remarkable. Just as expected, you have all of the markers of the genetic atavism," he said as he stared. "Blue-green eyes. Extra-long torso to accommodate the vestigial rib. Fascinating." His expression changed. "I'm sorry about your sister's passing. So unfortunate."

Her face and neck flushed red. "Don't talk about my sister."

Malcolm frowned and his furry grey eyebrows met in the middle, like caterpillars crawling together. "Modern medicine is so ill-equipped to cope with profoundly diverse biology. Although, I suppose considering the unlikely expression of your particular genome, one can hardly expect otherwise."

I lurched toward him, my fists clenched and ready, but the guards immediately moved to stand between us. I stopped, staring at him.

"A quick question, Adriana and Kalan," Malcolm said, refusing to acknowledge my hostility. "Does it tingle or burn when you come into contact with saliva, tears, or bodily fluids?"

My breath caught. How would he know such a thing? "I don't know what you're talking about," I said, lying. I hoped he wouldn't notice my racing heart rate.

Adriana's nostrils flared. "No."

"Hmm. Curious," Malcolm crossed the room to the desk and wrote something on a clipboard. "I would have expected with the high levels of energy in your combined mitochondria, any contact of bodily fluids would have been rather notable. Perhaps you've never had the opportunity to see. Oh, well, it's a simple enough test to run you both through."

"It burns," Marcus said, outing us. I cast a glare his way. "She bit me and it burned."

Malcolm smiled at Adriana. "Just as I thought."

"Are you going to tell us what you want?" Genevieve asked.

Malcolm sauntered around behind his desk once again. "In time, Genevieve. In time." He picked up the phone on his desk.

"Our guests are here. Are their quarters ready for them?" Malcolm spoke into the receiver. "Excellent." He hung up, motioned to the guards while addressing us as a group. "I'm certain you are all rather weary after today's events, so I've ensured your rooms are ready. I will be available for questions later."

The security team herded us toward the door. All of us, including Marcus.

Shock registered on Marcus's face. "Malcolm, I thought you said I didn't need to go—" Marcus stopped speaking when he saw Malcolm's dark glare.

Malcolm didn't respond to Marcus. "All of them."

Immediately, Marcus held up his hand, the gesture he'd used in the abandoned hotel right before he crushed everyone's throats. A strange electrical snap rang through the air and I involuntarily blinked.

When I opened my eyes, Marcus's hands were strung up behind his back, wrapped in a pulsating form, something that looked gelatinous in the interior with a clear membrane on the outside. The whole thing throbbed, and with every pulse, Marcus stiffened, as if he was being electrocuted. Was this some kind of conducted energy weapon, like a Taser?

Malcolm spoke to his guards with a mechanical coldness. "Knock that one out."

A club came down on the back of Marcus's head. He dropped to the floor like a rag doll. Malcolm observed his son's prone body on the floor with utter indifference. "That's for attempting escape," he said to his unconscious son. He looked up and stared at the rest of us. "Let that be a lesson to all of you. Attempts to disarm my guards or escape will be met with the highest level of force necessary." He pinned me with his gaze. "We are a state of the art laboratory, and we will not hesitate to ensure its security."

I held Malcolm's gaze as we were led away. He knew of our abilities and he was warning me not to use them. What exactly, did he know about us? How much of our abilities were actually traits that he had genetically selected? Did he know things about me that I hadn't yet discovered?

On the walk to our assigned rooms, my mother's voice entered my mind once again.

*"You're here to be experimented on. We all are."* She glanced over at the two guards dragging Marcus. *"Marcus has no idea what he's done. He thinks he's allied himself with Malcolm. But Malcolm is allied with no one. He's incapable of loyalty. The only thing he is committed to is his research. And his praises."*

*"How did this happen?"* I asked, without uttering a word. Adriana's teal eyes were fixed on the two of us, her eyes narrowed. Could she tell we were communicating?

*"I loved your father once. That was at a time when I didn't yet know who he was or what he was about. But by the time I figured it out, it was too late. I was already pregnant with you and*

*Marcus."*

Her eyes shone in the harsh lights. *"What are we, Marcus and I?"* I wasn't sure I wanted to know her answer.

*"I think you already know. You are an experiment. Started by Malcolm's father, and carried out by Malcolm."* One tear zigzagged down Genevieve's dirty cheek, leaving a pale stripe from her eye to chin. I felt a strange stab of sympathy for her. My mother.

The guards slowed to a stop when they reached the end of the hall where a floor-to-ceiling window looked out over a huge ravine. How big was this place? With stern looks, the guards pointed to four doors, two on one side of the hallway, two on the other.

"You, here," said one guard, a huge man who was shaved bald. He opened the door and waited for Genevieve to enter. She went in without incident. Then it was Adriana's turn. "Your room is here," he said. Adriana glared at him and then turned to face me. The fierce look in her eyes made me cringe.

"We'll figure this out," I said as she walked through the doors. Once inside, her mouth opened as if she was about to respond, but the guard shut the door in her face.

Marcus roused and looked at the guards. His head jerked back and forth, his eyes darting about. He'd expected to be in charge.

"And you. In here," a blond guard said to Marcus. He

pointed at the door beside Adriana's room.

Marcus stared. "You've got to be kidding. I brought them here."

The guard was unfazed. "In. Now."

Marcus struggled in his restraint. Despite the weapon appearing stretchy, it was obviously inflexible. Marcus turned on his heel and attempted to run, but all four guards grabbed him, one by his hair and one by his collar, the other two by his sleeves. They yanked him so hard he almost lost his footing while the see-through weapon re-activated, a series of shocks jolting through his body. Then they shoved him into the room with such force he fell on his face. Blood pooled beneath him. They slammed the door and locked it from the outside. My mouth went dry.

The blond guard turned to me. "Are you going put up a fight like your brother?"

I shook my head *no* and went in. The guard shut the door behind me, and the metallic clink that followed told me that I, too, was locked in from the outside.

The room was a perfect square. White concrete blocks made up all four walls. There were no windows, the only light from two rows of humming fluorescents overhead. A bed was situated directly in the middle of the room, an ivory knit coverlet on top, like what you would find in a hospital. There was a small opening into a bathroom on the left, and a jut-out closet on the right. Beside the bed was a small wooden side table with a lamp.

Underfoot, the flooring was gray, a stark contrast from the painted white concrete walls. The entire room was cold, but not because of the temperature. It was the icy sensation of being locked in this white and grey room, isolated and cut off from the outside world.

I focused and attempted to reach out to my mother.

*"Genevieve. Can you hear me?"*

I waited for the sound of her voice inside my mind. After at least a minute my head began to throb, my blood pressure escalating with effort. My eyes were undoubtedly haemorrhaging. *"Mother?"* A tinny squeal rang in my ear.

*"She can't hear you, Kalan. But I can."*

*"Marcus?"*

*"Yes."*

Was there anything my brother couldn't do? *"Marcus, what was that thing they used on you?"*

It was almost as if I could hear Marcus sigh. *"Malcolm knows about my abilities. He knows about you, too. He's always known. He engineered us this way."*

My skin felt icy. *"What was it? Some kind of Taser?"*

*"It appears to be, yes. It's some kind of electrically conductive plastic or maybe something else. It locks my muscles up and I'm rendered physically useless. As useless as you."*

Even though his voice wasn't being spoken out loud, I could hear the humiliation in my brother's words, beneath the sarcasm. *"I can't help but think you deserve this, Marcus. If you'd left everything alone, continued to work with me, and trust me to find our mother, this never would have happened. But you couldn't, could you? You can't let go of the fact that life was unfair to us."*

After several minutes, Marcus finally replied. *"It shouldn't have been that way."*

My patience ran out. *"I don't care what it should have been like. There's no guarantee life will be easy or good. Maybe you should ask our father if he selected traits that have made you so fucking self-absorbed and miserable!"*

Marcus didn't respond, and after about twenty minutes, I stopped waiting. I paced around and inspected my jail-cell of a room. What little there was of it.

The bathroom was no larger than the size of a stall at a roadside gas station, the toilet and sink nearly touching. The wooden closet held two hangers on the steel rod and nothing else. The bed, barely the width of a single mattress, was hard and unyielding, the blanket woollen and itchy. The side table had nothing but an old brass table lamp on top of it.

I looked under the bed. It too, was bare.

A crackling sound erupted inside of my room. The static echoed within the bare walls.

"In twenty minutes, you will be gathered together for preliminary testing," said a voice over the intercom. The static stopped. The word, testing, sounded very bad.

I began to pace.

#

We were gathered up like a herd of sheep and taken to an area that looked like a cross between a hospital room and a science lab. The presence of four tables/beds outfitted with maternity-style stirrups and an adjustable overhead light only served to make it look like a birthing room.

Even Marcus was ineffectual, his abnormal abilities prevented by the gelatinous-looking device wrapped around not only his wrists, but now also around his throat. If Malcolm knew how to stop Marcus, then he probably knew about everything we could do. And then what hope was there for us to get out of here?

Surrounded by guards, we waited. Malcolm entered the room. "Welcome back," he said with a smile. There was no warmth in that smile. The gap between his front teeth looked even more pronounced than what I remembered. "I realize none of you have eaten in some time, and undoubtedly you are growing hungry. However, before we have our meal, we need to get the preliminary tests underway. If we have reasonable cooperation, your experience here will be far quicker and much more pleasant."

"What are you testing for?" I asked.

"Ah, yes, Kalan. Excellent question." Malcolm stepped toward me, gap-toothed smile filling up his face. "We'll be performing a basic metabolic panel, molecular profile, cellular evaluation, the usual."

"What is it for?" I asked.

Malcolm laughed. "I suppose I shouldn't be surprised you're so quizzical. After all, your intelligence was selected for." Malcolm smirked and walked away. If only I had ten minutes alone with him.

"This is crazy," I said.

"I've been told that before. So, I suppose, despite the obvious cliché, there is a kernel of truth in the statement." Malcolm looked at Genevieve, his head angled to one side. "I believe it was your mother who made that proclamation, some twenty or so years previous to this day."

Genevieve held Malcolm's gaze, but said nothing.

"Okay." Malcolm clapped his hands together. "Enough. Let's begin," He nodded as if there was a small army of people waiting along the sidelines for his signal. There was. From two side doors flooded numerous people, some in lab coats, others in riot gear. They walked with purpose toward us and branched off to each individual. We each had one or more people assigned to us.

Two burly men grabbed my arms and pulled me forward while two women and a man in lab coats followed behind. A burning pain shuddered through my upper forearm and then in the soft spot behind my ear, where they gouged their thumbs into my flesh.

My knees buckled and they took the opportunity to twist me up like a pretzel.

Adriana struggled too, the same tactical techniques used on

her, except she screamed and kicked in defence. Marcus had a gun pushed up against his spine in addition to the transparent Taser around his wrists and neck. Genevieve went cooperatively to the examining table without a word and watched us in silence. Her face was the embodiment of pity.

The guards dragged me to an exam table. Behind me was the usual array of medical instruments, including oxygen, a blood pressure cuff, and other examination devices.

They strapped me down, the adjustable belts pulled tight across my chest, waist, wrists, upper thighs and ankles. I was immobile. A middle-aged woman with brown hair pulled into a tight bun slid a needle beneath my skin and removed two vials of my blood. She stuck a thermometer under my tongue. She pricked my finger with a tiny lance.

I heard Adriana's voice from across the room. "What are you doing to me?" she asked.

The nurse beside her responded robotically, "We're checking to see if you are ovulating."

*"THE AFFINITIES of all the beings of the same class have sometimes been represented by a great tree. I believe this simile largely speaks the truth."*
-Charles Darwin

## CHAPTER ELEVEN

### ADRIANA SINCLAIR

After the first round of tests I was released from the chair. With a security escort in tow, I was led by someone who appeared to be a nurse to a waiting room where I was told in a pointed tone by the guard to sit down and *not move*. He hovered two feet from me, watching to see if I would disobey. I did as I was told, and after twenty or so minutes, he stepped around the corner of the waiting room and out of his sight.

I tiptoed to the corner and glanced down the hall. The guard was standing in an open doorway, talking to someone. Their intermitted laughter echoed down the length of the hallway.

I went the opposite direction. Within a few steps I came to a conference room where I slowed down at the partially open door. I could hear a familiar voice inside the boardroom. I strained to listen, to recall the face behind the voice. Then it came to me. It was Dr. Bomer. One of the geneticists at NHGRI.

"Many colleagues believe our race was derived from a single decedent, one that lived over two hundred thousand years ago. But up until today, we had no evidence to prove our theory." There was a long pause. I stepped around so I could peer into the room through a gap in the door. There were other doctors in there that I recognized from the meeting with my mother at NHGRI.

"We believe Analiese is a genetic throwback to this original hominid," said a man with a gruff voice and a heavy Irish accent.

My heart thumped so hard it felt like it was in my throat.

"Actually," Dr. Bomer said, "We are considering the possibility that the mutation is a re-expression of the original mitochondria."

"Although the likelihood of that is one in twenty billion," Dr. Irish said. Was he challenging Dr. Bomer?

Dr. Bomer's response was instantaneous and cutting. "There are seven billion people on the planet, Dr. Halan."

"Highly implausible," Was Halan's response. Were they actually having a debate?

"The maximum energy potential was much stronger in the original mitochondrion. And now we have a *living* re-expression of the mitochondrion. Far better than a cadaver."

"The Endosymbiotic Theory has all but been completely discredited, Mark," Dr. Halan added.

All of a sudden my hackles rose. "What are you doing

here?" said a voice in my ear. My arms were twisted up behind my back, the force causing the sensation of prickles of heat to explode in my injured shoulder. I screamed as the guard half pushed, half dragged me back to the lab, kicking all the way.

My throat ached from yelling. It wasn't even five hours since they'd drained half my blood, and already I was getting hauled back into the lab. Every time I screamed, the guards' grip on my arm got tighter and their fingers dug into the skin of my arms and ribs even further. I shouted out as they strapped me down, even though I knew it was in complete futility.

The worst part was the realization that all of this could have been avoided. If I wasn't so needy, so emotionally dependent and starved for someone else to validate me and confirm my existence, I wouldn't be in this situation. I would have kept my distance from Kalan from the very start, but no, I latched onto him like a parasite. Why couldn't I stand on my own two feet? *Because I'm needy. That's why.*

Was all of this because I couldn't accept that Analiese was dead and face the future without her? Of course it was. I couldn't bear the thought of being alone. I couldn't accept that Analiese was dead. And I couldn't accept that Analiese betrayed me.

A woman in pink scrubs with eyes the colour of coffee grounds rolled an apparatus that looked like an ultrasound machine on casters over to my exam table. The nurse ignored me as she turned the contraption on. Her straw-coloured hair was pulled back into a severe bun, the effect making her eyebrows look like she was from the planet Vulcan. Was a tight bun part of the dress code for this place?

"What are you doing to me?" I asked with as much menace as I could muster.

The woman's face was expressionless, which only added to her alien characteristics. She ignored my question as if I hadn't even spoken at all. She pulled out a needle and, without warning, inserted it into the flesh at the crook of my elbow. It was nearly painless, her expertise and experience at her work readily evident. She pulled out a long tube with another needle attached to the end and set it beside me.

The doors of the lab opened. Kalan, three guards and Malcolm entered the lab. Kalan looked at me, strapped to the table, machines and gadgets all around me, and his face blanched. Then an expression of intense concentration took over.

The pressure inside my head changed and my ears popped.

*"Adriana. Can you hear me?"*

"Yes," popped out of my mouth before I could stop it. My mouth snapped shut. The nurse looked at me and her eyebrows shot up on her forehead, her first real expression.

*"Don't speak out loud. I'm talking to you inside your mind. Can you answer without speaking?"*

*"How are you doing this?"*

The guards led Kalan toward a side door, into a separate

room altogether.

*"That doesn't matter right now. I'm going to get us out of here. I want you to ask to use the washroom. Say you have to throw up. When they unstrap you, make a run for the outside door, okay?"*

I swallowed as the woman opened my hospital gown and squirted clear gel all over my abdomen. *"What about you?"*

*"Call to me with your thoughts. I'll be in here, but I'll hear you."*

*"Okay."*

Kalan disappeared into the side room and Malcolm closed the door behind him.

Immediately, I yelled out, "Ugh!" and leaned forward as far as my restraints would let me. "My stomach, it hurts. I think I'm getting my period. I feel like I'm going to throw up."

"That's not possible, you're ovulating," said Vulcan woman, her eyes narrowed.

I had to do something dramatic. I turned my head to the side and made retching noises, complete with spitting onto the floor. The woman wheeled her chair backward and stood up with a look of complete revulsion on her face. Her second real expression. She glanced around as if unsure what to do. Two guards rushed over as I moaned and continued to wretch. I cried out in choked gasps. I heaved for so long, my stomach churned and I actually threw up onto the floor. Spock lady's mouth dropped open and she ripped all of the attachments off me, including the needle from my elbow.

"Get her to the bathroom," she said to the guards. She waved her hand as if my germs dripped from her fingers.

They removed my straps, making no effort to do it gently. They did everything possible to avoid touching me or my vomit. Maybe I finally had the upper hand.

I retched once again, right onto their pants. A little got on their hands and sleeves. They yelled and jumped back as they yanked their hands away. I was almost free from the restraints, save for one strap that held down my right hand. I easily wriggled out of it and launched myself off the table. I was halfway to the door when the sounds of footsteps resonated behind me.

"Kalan! I'm at the door!"

The door burst open and Kalan ran out holding up his pants that were missing a belt. I held the door open for him while the guards ran to intercept us.

Kalan stopped and turned to stare at the guards. His eyes were wide and intense, and oddly, the guards stopped dead in their tracks. Their eyes widened, mouths open as if they were paralyzed.

What...?

I didn't have time to wonder. Kalan ran for the doorway and I followed. We took off down the hallway, our bare feet slap-slap-slapping against the cold tile.

I slowed as we approached an open door where I heard

several voices inside. I peered partway in, and saw a large table with chairs around it. A boardroom. I grabbed Kalan's arm and stopped him. If we ran past, we'd only alert even more people to our missing whereabouts.

I was about to run the opposite direction when I heard Malcolm's voice, loud and clear, his English accent making him sound haughty and self-aggrandized. "Her DNA is not a throwback at all," Malcolm said with unrestrained contempt. "It is re-expression of the original DNA, evolved once again to its maximum potential. Again to a time of early symbiosis. The energy potential of the mitochondria in those three is so advanced we cannot even begin to estimate its influence on gene sequencing."

"Isn't there a chance the embryos will have negative recessive traits? We are talking about two generations of consanguinity, Malcolm," said another voice.

Consanguinity. I knew this term from biology. In layman's terms it meant inbreeding. Two generations of inbreeding.

Now Malcolm's tone was beyond contempt. I could imagine the sneer on his face. "Of course they will. That's why we'll select the zygotes we wish to proceed."

"You'll dispose of the rest, then?"

"No." Malcolm's voice. "We'll harvest them for parts. I'm certain we can learn from their physiology. They don't need to be sentient, of course, because that would be unethical," he chuckled.

"But they don't need brains to be of use to our research."

My skin went cold. He was completely self-focused, intent on what would be of use for him, and him alone. Did he not have a fatherly bone in his entire body? Didn't he look at Kalan and Marcus and have even a twinge of loving emotion? Or did he see them as mere specimens? Grown up zygotes? *We'll harvest them for parts.* I shivered.

"Just imagine the press release where I reveal what I've created. First, Adriana, the Mitochondrial Eve. Then, the fathers, Marcus and Kalan, the Adam Chromosomes, and finally, the newest offspring," he paused. Then with great theatre, he said, "The God Sequence."

I was literally vibrating now, every muscle twitching. I forgot to breath. My lungs screamed for oxygen. Kalan grabbed my arm and pulled me in the opposite direction. We'd listened too long, our window of opportunity to escape rapidly closing. We broke out in a run.

The heavy footsteps behind us underscored my words. We picked up speed, but as we came to a point in the hall that split off into three curved hallways, we stopped.

"This way," Kalan said and we veered into the hall on the left.

An alarm started. At the other end of the hallway two guards ran toward us. I hesitated, but Kalan didn't slow his pace. Then, Kalan held his arms out in a stop gesture. Like in the lab, the guards went immobile.

We picked up speed and barrelled past the guards who watched in their helpless, frozen state. We reached an exit. Kalan shoved the crash bar of the door with his shoulder but the massive double doors didn't budge. They were locked.

"Goddamn it!" Kalan yelled. He glanced around, his eyes wild.

"If you can stop them in their tracks like that, then we can go through the front entrance where we came in," I said.

Kalan's lips pursed as he contemplated it, and then nodded. "Right. Let's try."

My heels burned from running in bare feet. The whole building was like a damn maze. We reached the massive open foyer of the entrance. Faint classical music was heard, barely audible beneath the sound of the screeching alarm.

There was a flurry of activity. People scurried about at faster than normal speeds but in deliberate, controlled movements. Kalan pointed to a door beneath the staircase that led outside.

"That door. Maybe it's unlocked."

I grabbed Kalan's hand and we ran down the stairs, two at a time.

We crashed through the door, immediately plunged into inky darkness of nightfall. It took several moments to regain my bearings. When I did, I realized we were surrounded by a number of small buildings.

"There," I said. I pointed to where the road snaked between the buildings, toward what looked vaguely like a wrought iron gate.

We ran down the road, the rocks and gravel grinding into my feet. It felt like I was walking on razor blades. I tried to steel myself against the pain, but the jagged stones were so sharp in the soft flesh of my feet I couldn't stop the odd gasp from sounding.

I glanced over and saw the grimace on Kalan's face, he was struggling too. Speedy healing didn't mean pain reduction.

There was no sound, a reprieve from the alarms, only the slight hum from one overhead light. All of the buildings were closed, no lights on inside. Crickets chirped, lending an eerie, isolated feel to the situation. Even the moon was a half-crescent, doing nothing to improve my visual acuity.

We neared the gate, and when we did, a loud, electrical whine started up, followed by the whir of mechanical hydraulics.

The gate was closing.

We took off in a flat-out sprint, the gate almost halfway closed. Never had I run so hard in my life, every muscle in my legs ached, my feet burned and an odd metallic taste filled my mouth.

As we grew closer, I knew. It was too late.

The opening between the gates had less than the width of a person between them. Kalan grabbed the gate and shoved against it, using his upper body to push against the movement. But it was useless. The iron came together with a resounding clang.

The height was twelve or more feet, and the retaining wall beside it was solid concrete. There was no possibility of scaling the wall.

I tried to catch my breath. Kalan's eyes were wild, the silvery sheen flashing near-white in the minimal light. There was nowhere else to run. The sound of footsteps in gravel grew closer. We were about to be discovered. Kalan pointed to a building.

We took off for it. When Kalan pulled on the door, it was open. We went into the storage space where boxes and boxes were stacked one on top of the other, the skull and crossbones sign prominently displayed on each and every box. In another corner were shelves with innumerable yellow plastic bins with "Biohazard" written on them. Old computer monitors sat in the middle of the space, as well as large blue plastic tubs with the word "Flammable" all over them.

Kalan grabbed my hand and led me to the farthest back corner where he found a ladder. He turned to me, and there must have been something he saw in my face, because he let go of the ladder and pulled me to him. I put my arms around his neck and he folded me into his chest. Immediately, our heartbeats combined to make an irregular, frantic thumping, our breaths still coming in great gasps.

Kalan kissed me, his lips closed. "You heard them in there, and what Genevieve said. They're going to use you, like my mother. They want your genetic material as a base."

"A base." A lump formed in my throat. "For what?"

"I think she was right. He wants to genetically engineer a person, selecting for what he thinks are perfect traits."

The ends of my fingers tingled. "Why? The perfect human, like Genevieve said? To engineer a freak and finally be good enough?"

Kalan nodded his head. "And because he has a God complex. Father issues and something to prove. He wants to do it, and he wants the fame and recognition for achieving it. So he's going to go through with it, no matter who gets hurt."

A string of curses erupted from my mouth. They stopped as soon as Kalan kissed me again, and this time, the kiss was long, and desperate, as if we may never see each other again. I never wanted this moment to end, being held tight against him, his strong arms holding me as we hid from the horrible realities of the world. Consanguinity or not, I felt for this man.

Kalan pulled away, but his mouth hovered right in front of mine, so close, his hot breath touched my cheeks. "I'll have to kill him. Maybe then we'll have a fighting chance at getting out of here. Listen for my cue. I won't be speaking it out loud."

"When did you realize you could do that? Speak mind to mind?" I asked. I ran a hand through his downy-soft hair. Would I ever get to touch his hair again?

Kalan shrugged. "My mother did it when we left the hotel. She told me there's more to my ability, but I need to be open to discovering it. That's what I'm trying to do. It appears there is a lot more to my abilities than I've ever allowed myself to accept."

"Like stopping those guards in the hall?" I asked.

"Yes," Kalan said.

"What about that weapon he used against Marcus? Will it work on you, too?"

He contemplated my question. "I don't know. Probably." He grabbed the ladder again and started toward the door. "Come on. I don't want to find out."

As if his last words were a premonition, the door to the building crashed open, the entire space lit up with the strobe effect of numerous flashlights. We ducked behind the blue plastic containers, but the heavy footfalls closed in on us.

Kalan grasped my hand and tugged back along the wall and toward the entrance.

My collar suddenly closed in around my throat as a fist jabbed into my back. The voice was cold and toneless behind me. "Stop moving."

#

This time I knew there would be no faking sick and attempting escape. Now there were four guards escorting me back, all of them the largest I'd seen yet, my hands cuffed behind my back. I resigned myself to whatever unpleasant and possibly painful procedure they would perform.

The hulking men led me back to the same lab, with the

same nurse, who had the same extreme bun, but this time, she was wearing lime green scrubs instead of pink. And while she maintained the mechanical way of going about her job, she now had a cold edge in every glance and mannerism. She also seemed to be taking less care in being gentle, and when she shoved the needle into my arm, I yelped. All four guards stood around the table and watched my every move, ready to act at the slightest provocation.

The nurse lowered the table so I was horizontal and pushed my medical gown up to my armpits, my bare lower half fully exposed. I squeezed my eyes shut.

*"As genetics allows us to turn the tide on human disease, it's also granting the power to engineer desirable traits into humans. What limits should we create as this technology develops?"*
*-Nature.com*

## CHAPTER TWELVE

### KALAN KANE

I went with the guards without putting up a fight because I wanted to save my energy for when it counted. For Adriana. Besides, I didn't know what my father was aware of, in terms of my abilities, and the more I could surprise them at the last minute, the better.

But watching them yank Adriana's slender arms high behind her back and the pained expression that followed was nearly too much. If she'd cried out, I wouldn't have been able to hold back, but thankfully, she hadn't.

Now, inside my room, I was once again cut off from everyone. Like a caged animal, I wanted to climb the walls. How long would it take before Malcolm came to address me? I didn't want to think about what would happen when that moment came to pass. Feeling helpless and ramped up, overfilled with nervous energy I couldn't bleed off, I sat down on the bed and focused on reaching out to my mother.

*"Mother. Can you hear me?"* I waited, but there was no response. I called to her once again. Nothing.

Then a familiar voice streaked through my mind.

*"So you and Adriana made a run for it?"* Marcus's voice.

I ignored the surge of anger that ran through me. *"This place is like a fortress. There's no way out."*

Marcus's sarcastic tone came through loud and clear, despite the fact that his words weren't even spoken aloud. *"I could have told you there was no way out. Saved you the energy."* I could imagine Marcus's smirk. *"I've been here before."*

Now it was my turn to be snide. *"Well done. You've managed to bring us to him and lead yourself into imprisonment in the process. Very wise, brother."*

Marcus didn't respond right away. *"I had no idea he would turn on me."*

*"This man used his own genetic material to engineer us. We are scientific specimens to him, that's all. What kind of person did you think he was?"* I asked.

*"I underestimated. Obviously."* Marcus's answer was diminutive.

*"Obviously."* I flopped back on my bed, overwhelmed at the ridiculousness of my brother's stupidity. *"How much does Malcolm know about you—and your abilities? How did he know to make that weapon?"*

*"He knows everything."*

I pressed my knuckles into my eye sockets and punched the wall. My knuckles crunched with the impact of skin and bone against concrete. *"Fuck. You're stupid. Do you know that?"* When Marcus didn't respond, I continued. *"Why did you do this, Marcus? Why did you put us in this situation?"*

There was such a long pause I almost thought he wasn't going to answer at all. *"He's our father. I wanted to believe what he said, that it was genuine. To have us all reunited."*

*"And you thought by forcing us, we would embrace the reunification?"*

Marcus paused again. *"He told me Genevieve was crazy. Paranoid and delusional. When I saw her, living like that, I thought he was right. He said I'd have to force her."*

*"And what about me and Adriana? Did he say you'd have to force us, too?"*

*"He said to do whatever was necessary to bring you in,"* Marcus said. *"And I was angry at you for keeping the information about our mother from me."*

I punched the wall. Was he so desperate for parental love and acceptance that he actually led us all into this? *"I need to know precisely what he knows. It's the only way we'll defeat him."*

Marcus laughed. *"How is that, exactly?"*

*"Because. I've finally accepted the truth, and now that I have, I'm developing new abilities every time I turn around. If I*

*don't even know about them, how could he? Maybe if we have something unexpected to use against him, we'll have a fighting chance."*

Marcus hesitated and then answered. *"Okay. I'll tell you everything."*

#

There were six guards who came to retrieve me this time. Obviously they weren't taking any chances. I supposed I should have been flattered, but all I could think about was how much more difficult it would be to outwit and physically overwhelm all six of them at once. They led me to a side room where I was instructed to put on a hospital gown. I refused. To my surprise, they walked away and left me alone. To wait.

After a few minutes, a man in white scrubs approached me, those same guards following beside him. The lab man's hair was greyish-white and he peered at me with dark blue eyes. They looked like two ripe blueberries set in a ruddy face of broken capillaries.

"What is this I hear? You're refusing to cooperate?" He spoke in a loud, jovial manner, like some sobering Santa Claus, annoyed I wouldn't get up onto his knee.

I glared at him. "I want to know what you're doing."

The man's eyebrows lowered in the middle. "We need a semen sample."

I cursed, and he backed up as guards simultaneously moved

toward me.

"Obviously, I'm not going to cooperate," I said, my voice a low growl.

He laughed. His belly jiggled. Like a bowl full of jelly. "There are ways to attain a sample that don't require your cooperation."

I swallowed. "What the hell does that mean?"

"It's difficult to explain without sounding crass." The man smiled. "I can use a sedative, if you'd prefer. It will help you relax."

"I guess I'm going down fighting," I said as I lunged at the guards and they tackled me to the ground.

#

Malcolm lined us up, side by side, each with at least one guard behind us. The skin on my face burned from the humiliating experience I'd just undergone, and my entire body was still shaking. I was situated beside Adriana, and Malcolm made no move to stop us from holding hands. Her palm felt cold and clammy, matching the greyish cast to her complexion. I'd never seen her look so pale.

On my other side stood my mother, who had yet to respond to my silent questions. Beyond her was Tait, who looked dumbfounded, his eyes still black and blue from getting thumped over the head and hitting the ground face-first. Beside him, furthest from me, was Marcus.

My brother no longer had his usual smug, arrogant look. In fact, his entire body emanated defeat, from the sloped quality of his shoulders, to his downcast eyes. If I didn't know better, I'd almost feel sorry for him. But Karma was a bitch.

What made Marcus look all the more pathetic were his attempts to touch Tait's hand, and Tait's repeated rebuffs. After about three attempts on the part of Marcus, Tait folded his arms across his chest. I guess mind control was no longer working for Marcus.

I glanced back at the row of guards. Each of them had lengths of the transparent weapon they'd used on Marcus, the sci-fi gadget hanging from their gun belts like whips made of slimy rubber. What other high-tech devices did my father have in store for us?

The room was silent as we waited for the self-acclaimed Science God to walk in. I was fast learning that my father enjoyed an audience.

Malcolm strode in, followed by several people in white lab coats who trailed behind him like parasitic minions. He wore jeans and a collared shirt, his lab coat open in the front. The scientists around him had their white lab coats buttoned all the way up, their name tag lanyards dangled around their necks, blue rubber gloves tucked into their breast pockets. Did they all signed non-disclosure contracts to work here? Or was the threat of being the next lab rat enough to keep them silent and compliant?

"I have brought you all here today to outline the requirements of the next several months. I also wanted to give you the opportunity to say good-bye to your loved ones, as you will be separated from this point on." He looked directly at me. "It appears I've been far too trusting."

Genevieve spoke first. "Malcolm, what do you want with me? I'm old. I can't reproduce for you anymore. Surely I'm only taking up space."

Malcolm strode over to Genevieve and looked at her with a kind of tenderness. "I want you to be here for it. To be present for what we've created, you and I. Our collective offspring. Unfortunately, you are correct about your lack of value to me. Preliminary results from Adriana's tests indicate the energy within her mitochondria is far beyond yours."

"What you are doing is wrong, Malcolm, and you know it." Genevieve's voice was soft and intimate, as if Malcolm was her one and only true love.

Malcolm's expression fell, as if she'd slapped him in the face. "No, Jennie. Human weakness and inconsistencies can be fixed. It is simply the rate of advancement in molecular genetics surpassing that of natural selection. I'm merely hastening the process."

Genevieve shook her head as her eyes filled with tears. "No, Malcolm. You can't tamper with nature this way. You are not God."

Malcolm's brow furrowed. "God? This has nothing to do with creationism. My lab has made the speed of genome sequencing increase exponentially. And do you know why? It is not because of a god, but because of people, who have made computers so advanced our ability to sequence genomes is growing ever faster. Don't you see? Imagine how this will open up enormous vistas for biological research and create astonishing changes in human medicine." He crossed his arms in front of his chest, his eyes narrowed. "Look at them." He gestured to me and Marcus with an odd kind of reverence. "Do you see what this lab made possible? Science did that. Not God. And I will forever be known as the geneticist who created *them*."

Tears streaked down my mother's face. Her voice rang out inside my head. *"I'm sorry for what I'm about to say, Kalan."*

She took a step toward Malcolm but guards grabbed each of her arms and stopped her. "Are you talking about Marcus? The infant who came out screaming and went on to become a vengeful, hostile young man, whose only use of his genetically engineered strengths are used for selfish reasons? Or do you mean Kalan, who looks like he was meant to live in a bubble and who obviously doesn't even feel comfortable in his own skin?"

I swallowed, now understanding why she apologized to me before she spoke. And yet, every word she said was true.

Malcolm's eyes narrowed. "That's precisely why we need to finish our research. Prototypes always have errors."

Genevieve wiped away her tears and gaped at Malcolm, her whole body shaking. "They are not goddamn prototypes, Malcolm! They're people!" Her face turned beet red, eyes flashing. Then her face went slack and she clutched her chest, right before her knees buckled and her body crumpled to the ground.

"Genevieve!" Malcolm jumped forward in an attempt to catch her, but missed. Her head hit his shoe. He dropped to his knees and pulled her onto his lap to check her throat for a pulse. She blinked at him, her mouth open as she sucked in shallow breaths. He waved frantically at the guards behind him. "Page the physician."

Two guards came to her side, and Malcolm helped them hoist her into one of the guard's arms. They swept her out of the room. The door slammed shut behind them. Now, Malcolm looked rattled. When he addressed us this time, he was noticeably quieter, his expression far more serious.

"Genevieve's contribution to Project Eve is complete. That's the last time you'll see her. I'm sorry you weren't able to say goodbye."

My mouth dropped open. "What? What do you mean, that's the last time we'll see her? Where in the hell are you taking her?"

Malcolm looked down, and for a second, I wondered if his expression showed a hint of...regret? "I'm afraid Genevieve has always been a liability. I've been searching for her for years, only recently coming anywhere close to finding her. And for that,

Marcus, I am eternally grateful."

Marcus's face was ashen. Tait stood beside him with a look of equal parts disgust and horror.

Marcus spoke. "You're not going to kill her, are you?"

Malcolm's eyebrows rose in the middle as he registered his son's reaction. "What is this, Marcus? A radical change in conscience?"

Tait shuffled sideways, further from Marcus, and eyed him with unmuted disdain. Marcus caught the look, and his entire expression darkened. Tait's glare must have been his breaking point. Without hesitation, Marcus launched himself at Malcolm and tackled him to the floor. The guards sprang to life and were immediately at their boss's side, but it was too late. Marcus had our father in a headlock.

"Touch me with that thing so my muscles lock up, and his carotid will experience the full extent of my muscle rigidity." Marcus's lip was curled back, his eyes glittering like black diamonds.

My brother's voice entered my mind. *"I'll take these guards. You take the ones behind you."*

*"Okay."*

I whipped around and without thinking, grabbed Adriana and put her in a headlock. Her eyes flashed. *"I'm sorry,"* I said, mind to mind. She squeaked but didn't respond.

"The same is true for me," I said to the guards. Their

shocked expressions and tightly coiled muscles hovered over the translucent weapons. Seeing their fingers twitch gave me the courage to continue. "You need her. You take me out and she's gone."

They looked to Malcolm for direction, but he was unable to speak. His eyes bulged, staring at them, silently willing them to do something to help him, but unable to communicate with words. The irony.

When the guards remained in their unmoving state of indecision, Marcus stood up and carefully pulled Malcolm upright with him. The guards cringed, obviously at a loss about what to do as they observed their boss gasp for air. I backed up with Adriana in my hold, struggling to ensure she could breathe freely while making it look convincing that I was a hair's width away from cutting off her oxygen. Tait came with us, despite the wide-eyed look on his face.

A croaking sound erupted from Malcolm's mouth and his skin turned a deep shade of burgundy.

"Let go of him!" The guard yelled, pulling the gun from the holster in his belt. "I can still shoot you in the leg!"

Marcus smiled and his nostrils flared, his lips curled back in a snarl. "Try it. I'll squeeze that much harder on my way down."

The guards didn't move. Their eyes were as wide as saucers, beads of sweat dripping from their foreheads.

"Let's go," I said. We backed up toward the closest door.

Tait held the door open for Marcus, who steered Malcolm forward, his throat still at the crook of his elbow. As soon as the door was closed behind us I let go of Adriana. "Are you okay?" I asked. She nodded. I grasped a steel bar from a side lab and fed it through the door handles to keep the guards locked-in.

Marcus led with Malcolm in front, in his vulnerable position. They walked with purpose, and after rounding several corners, reached the main foyer where people milled about, unaware of what was going on. The entire room fell silent.

Shouting broke out and guards ran toward us as people in lab coats ran away. Marcus stopped. "I'll kill him if any one of you takes even one step!" he yelled.

They all, save for one, stopped. A tall bald man with a black goatee continued forward toward Marcus. Even from my vantage point I could see Marcus squeeze Malcolm's head in the bend of his arm. Malcolm's face turned purple-red and his knees buckled.

Everyone came to a sudden stop, including the guard with the goatee. Now we had a clear exit. We went for it.

I shoved my shoulder against the door, but it held firm. "What the—"

Marcus said, "There's a buzzer behind the front desk that will let us out."

I rushed over to the desk and jumped over it to push the button. The locks clicked, and Marcus shoved Malcolm through the doors and out into the night.

Adriana held her hand out to me. I could see in her expression that she understood my previous actions. I hopped back over the desk, took her hand, and together we entered the darkness beyond.

#

"Tait. You drive," Marcus barked out. He shoved our father into the back of the car headfirst. Momentum and the combined weight of their bodies resulted in Marcus and Malcolm falling into the backseat. Marcus righted himself, and adjusted so our father's throat was firmly in the crook of his arm. By now, Malcolm's face had turned a strange shade of purple, which made him look even more ghoulish in the dim interior car light. "The keys are in my back pocket."

Tait grabbed the keys from Marcus's pocket and hopped into the driver's seat. I pulled Adriana onto my lap in the front.

A red exterior light on the Eros building started to flash, followed by a wailing alarm bell.

"Hurry!" I said.

Tait turned the ignition on and the car roared to life. He shoved it in reverse, backed up, and then pushed it in drive. The tires squealed against the pavement.

A set of unnaturally-bright, huge headlights veered down the parking lot toward us.

Tait pulled a hard right. My head slammed into the

passenger side window. Pain burst through my temple, and everything went blurry. Adriana shifted in my lap, and I protectively tightened my hold to keep the same thing from happening to her.

Tait drove through the parking lot at top speed, hitting speed bumps so hard it made my teeth rattle. I glanced back. A huge black vehicle, something so big and square it resembled a black army tank, was bearing down on us, and judging by how close the headlights were, it was gaining ground. Fast.

The engine of Marcus's car roared, lurching up and down like a roller coaster ride, the back and forth momentum sending us sliding in our seats. The whole vehicle jarred forward, rammed from behind. The rending crunch of metal against metal groaned through the interior. Involuntarily, I braced myself and Adriana from hitting the dashboard, and pain shuddered through my wrist. Yells erupted from within the vehicle as we were bashed forward once again, our voices cut off from the impact.

"Take a hard right!" Marcus yelled from the backseat.

The massive black push-bumper on the front of the assaulting vehicle came at us once again, and the trunk space crumpled inward. My head flung sideways as Tait turned the steering wheel and floored the accelerator. The car lurched, almost as if it were going to end up on two tires, but continued on in a skid. I glanced back. The headlights were no longer behind us.

"Take another hard right and go back toward Eros," I said.

"They'll never expect us to go back there."

Tait did as I suggested, and as we approached Eros, my hands and feet turned clammy.

Then he turned left, away from the lab once again and drove the car to its limit. The black vehicle was nowhere to be seen.

It wasn't until after forty minutes of driving in silence that we stopped checking over our shoulders. My muscles slowly began to unclench. Behind me was a series of gasping breaths as Marcus let go of the sleeper hold. Malcolm sat more upright, but was still within Marcus's grip.

"What was that machine?" I demanded, glaring at my father. "An armoured vehicle?"

Malcolm opened and closed his mouth, like a guppy. He pulled at Marcus's forearm. Marcus loosened his grasp just enough so Malcolm could speak. "That's correct. An armoured vehicle." His voice was hoarse and gravelly. "Our facility is fully serviced with all scientific advancement, including military. We've been preparing for this day for some time."

My response was icy. "Not prepared well enough."

"Apparently not."

"Did you honestly think you could genetically engineer two physically and cognitively superior humans and not be outwitted by them?" Marcus sounded feral. "Your God complex has clearly reached the point of weakness."

"I think you are correct, my son—" Malcolm's response was immediately cut off and replaced by a gurgle as Marcus squeezed his father's throat in the crook of his elbow.

"Don't call me son!" Marcus yelled from the backseat.

Tait startled and glanced back. What was he feeling toward Marcus? Contempt? Hate?

"Are we going to kill him?" I asked. I could hardly believe the words were out of my mouth, so easily spoken. I glanced at Adriana. Her expression was stoic.

"Yes," Marcus said.

Malcolm gurgled and stuttered the odd groan. After at least a minute of this, Marcus let him speak.

"But you need me," Malcolm said with a gasp.

"For what?" Marcus snapped.

"Because I have Adriana's embryos."

#

We arrived at a motel for the night and even after a twenty minute shower, I couldn't stop shaking. I came out of the bathroom to find the room empty. Where was Adriana? I checked my cell. Her message read: *Getting ice. Right back.*

I threw a clean pair of jeans on and a t-shirt and went to the kitchenette area of the room. Inside the cutlery drawer was only one knife, a tiny paring knife that would do little damage. Unless it was used strategically. It would be enough to injure. I slipped it into my back pocket and left the room before Adriana returned.

I went into Marcus's room adjacent to ours. Marcus agreed to keep watch over Malcolm, with Tait keeping watch over Marcus. The two king-size beds were enough room to accommodate them, with Malcolm tied up and secured to a chair. I checked the ties, pulling at the ones around Malcolm's wrists attached at the back of his chair. They were so tight the skin above his hands was red and bulging. Marcus had done a good job. I glared down at Malcolm.

"Do you have any idea the pain you've caused us? Do you have any idea who you've hurt and sacrificed, so you could test out your hypothesis?" Malcolm looked up at me with wide eyes, a vein standing out in his forehead. When he didn't respond, I went on. "You took everything from Genevieve. She had to spend her entire life in hiding, to stay away from you. You went ahead and turned Marcus and I into freaks. Did you have any idea what that was like? To grow up a mutant—mocked by everyone you know? Mistrusted by even your own family?"

Malcolm didn't respond.

"Family. I suppose I shouldn't use that term so loosely. I was brought up in foster care, and Marcus was raised by individuals who merely wanted a doll to look at, a marionette they could be puppet master to, not a child to love."

Malcolm spoke, his voice uncharacteristically quiet. "It wasn't supposed to be that way. We were supposed to be a family, you, Marcus, your mother and I. She ruined it all. Genevieve is to blame for the way things have gone wrong."

My entire body shook and I ground my teeth together to keep from hitting him. "You don't get it, do you? You can't make people do things against their will! You can't just... rape people to get what you want!"

I shoved the chair with the sole of my foot and it momentarily tipped back on two legs before crashing back down onto all four. Malcolm's neck jerked and his mouth dropped open with the impact. I held the hilt of the knife in my clenched fist and my arm twitched.

I pushed the paring knife back down, into my pocket. If we had any hope of saving Genevieve and retrieving the fertilized eggs before they were harvested, we had to keep Malcolm alive, at least temporarily. *I don't care if you are my father. I just really, really want to kill you.*

I took a deep breath to stop myself from doing anything else. Knowing Adriana was probably waiting for me in the adjacent room kept me from rearing back and punching Malcolm in the jaw, or worse, slitting his throat from ear to ear. Instead, I pivoted on my foot so my back was to Malcolm. Tait and Marcus sat at opposite ends of the room. The tension between them was almost tangible, the atmosphere icy and caustic.

A cold war.

I needed to get out of this room. Now. "He's in your hands." I strode to the door.

Tait stood up and caught my arm and whispered into my ear. "Check on me, okay? What if he puts me under another one of his... spells?"

Marcus responded before I could. "It's called mind manipulation, Tait. No witchcraft involved. And I won't. You have my word." To my surprise, Marcus looked appropriately sheepish.

Tait rolled his eyes. "And I should believe *your* word?"

Marcus tilted his head to the side and smiled, no longer looking at all humble. "That's all you've got, isn't it, sweetheart?"

Tait's lips pressed into a hard line. "Kalan?"

"I'll check on you," I said.

I stepped out and closed the door behind me. I felt a strange tightening in my gut. Was it frustration that I couldn't kill my father? That I had to trust Marcus wasn't going to betray me once again? Or was it apprehension about being alone with Adriana, after what had happened to me in the lab? As I approached our room and pulled out the key card, I took a deep, steadying breath. I opened the door.

She sat on the bed, her feet dangling above the floor. Her black hair was still wild and dishevelled, a purple bruise flowered on her temple, her clothes rumpled. But the smile on her face made all of that disappear. She stood up and threw her arms around me in a tight embrace. I leaned into her, taking in the scent of her hair, blood and sweat mixed with her own unique raspberry fragrance.

I pulled away and looked down at her. "You heard what

Genevieve said about being a clone of Virginia and the stuff about consanguinity. We're cousins."

She blinked like I'd waved a fist in her face. "So what?"

"Third cousins, I think."

Adriana took a deep breath. "I just escaped a place where they'd finished inserting giant needles into my body to extract my ova so they could be fertilized by your sperm. Do you think I give a shit about whether we are third cousins right now?"

I bit my lip to keep from laughing. Right now she looked and sounded like the embodiment of the term *wild woman*. "Okay."

"Well, I guess I want to be with my third cousin right now." She set her hands on her waist and thrust one hip out. "Because I've just had a gun pointed at me, both of my legs spread wide open and strapped to stirrups for the entire room to see, and all the while I thought I was going to die. But I didn't. I escaped. Forgive me if I'm not feeling particularly concerned about the moral and ethical issues of being in love with my third cousin. I'm more focused on how I'm not dead."

"Enough said." I grabbed her roughly, and her body melded to me. She raised herself onto her tiptoes, her mouth on mine, the pressure enough to part my lips. Then her tongue was in my mouth and her hands slid up my back, her fingers woven through my hair. The familiar tingle in my mouth and lips began once again. It was a pleasure and pain I was becoming intensely addicted to.

I lowered her to the bed and she moaned as my body came to rest on top of hers. Our mouths were hot, our movements pressured, all of the tension and anxiety of the last days finally coming unravelled. She pulled my shirt up and over my head, and I tore it the rest of the way off.

Within moments I had her button-down top off so we were flesh to flesh again.

"Oh, Kalan," she whispered, her hot breath tickling my ear. "I thought we'd never be together, ever again."

"I know." Every nerve ending inside of me animated.

Adriana whispered into my ear. "I want you."

Even if I spent my entire lifetime with this woman, I could never get enough of her. I held her tiny waist, where the seventh rib was located, right above the flare of her hips. An unwanted image flashed through my mind, of being in the lab, my body violated in ways that before this, I could never have imagined. Instantly, the desire slipped from me as if I'd been plunged into an icy ocean. *No!*

Adriana seemed not to notice. I looked at her partially open mouth, full lips flushed pink. I loved her and wanted her, and forced myself with every inch of my being to hold the memory down, to damn it into the recesses of my mind.

What if I couldn't maintain my hold over these unwanted thoughts? For a moment, I wasn't sure my fears could be contained. Then I shoved it back and focused on loving her. A savage need to dominate took over all rational thought as if the movements of my body could keep the pain of the memory that clawed at the back of my mind at bay. I twined my fingers through her hair and pulled her head back roughly. She gave me the sweetest smile, a smile that spoke a thousand words.

*Holy shit.* I sucked in a heavy breath as my heart did a backflip. At no other time in my life had I felt like this, so cared for, accepted, like I was the most important person in Adriana's world. Her energy was like a healing blanket, the intimacy between us rebuilding and regenerating my trampled spirit. Never had I felt so whole, like I was... worthy. Was it like this for other people? Do other people's hearts feel like they're busting out of their chests when the person they love smiles at them in that way?

Then it hit me. I was in love with Adriana. The thought crossed my mind before, but now, I was acknowledging it to myself. Now it was different. Real.

"Wait," I said. She gasped, her mouth open. I gazed down at her and kissed the tip of her nose and swept stray hair back from her face "I've never met anyone like you," I said. "I don't want to rush this. We're under so much stress right now. We've been through so much. I don't think this is the right time. I want it to be... special." Silence ensued. I wondered what she was thinking.

Finally, she nodded. "Okay." She snuggled into me and her warm body softened to mine. We lay together like that for several minutes. "What's going to happen to those embryos?" Adriana asked.

My jaw clenched at just the thought of it. "I don't know."

Her eyes filled with tears, causing them to turn a most lustrous, brilliant shade of turquoise. "I can't stand the thought of our children... being out there without us to protect them. We can't let that happen, Kalan..." She trailed off, unable to finish her sentence. Two fat tears slid down her cheeks.

I swiped them off with my thumb and noted the warm sting on my skin. "We won't let that happen. I promise."

Adriana took two deep breaths. She held my hand up for her inspection, obviously taking in the slightly redder skin of my thumb.

"I'm sorry," she said. "I wish that didn't happen to you."

"Don't be sorry. I like it." I paused. "I wonder how Malcolm knew about the burning?"

She shook her head. "How many of them do you think there are? Embryos, I mean?"

The thought of it sickened me. "I have no idea. God, the thought of it is too... repulsive."

Adriana nodded. "How did they get your...?"

I stiffened as the physiological sensation of violation flooded my mind. Every muscle in my body tensed, like an over-tightened guitar string. "I don't think I can talk about it." My voice came out strange and raspy.

Adriana's eyes widened, her eyebrows high on her

forehead. Somehow, her concern only seemed to deepen my inner shame and horror. "Oh, God. I'm so sorry."

I squeezed my eyes shut and wished I could forcibly expel the memories from my cranium, reverse time to five minutes ago before she realized what had happened to me.

Adriana's soft fingertips brushed over my lips, my nose, my eyebrows. I kissed her. Finally, my body fully relaxed. I forced the memories back down and tried to focus on the here and now. I couldn't change the past and I didn't know what tomorrow would bring, but for the moment, I was at peace.

I didn't think I couldn't say it out loud yet, but I felt compelled to say it anyway. Even if it was mind to mind. *I think I love you, Adriana Sinclair.*

She smiled. *I think I love you, too, Kalan Kane.*

I slept.

#

A loud bang on the wall sounded from Marcus and Tait's room. Adriana and I both sat up.

The room was dim but bright light shone in under the curtains covering the window. Was it morning already? I got up and slipped into my jeans and t-shirt and Adriana followed. We hurried out to find the cause of the commotion.

The motel door to Marcus and Tait's room was locked, but the banging continued.

I knocked firmly but not too loud. I didn't want to alert

anyone in the motel. "Tait, what's going on?"

Tait opened the door, black rings beneath his eyes. "Your father has decided to be an enormous pain in the ass. He kept us up almost all night." He threw open the door and gestured dramatically toward Malcolm. Marcus stood over him, a thumb thrust into the side of our father's neck.

"Shut up or I'll give you something to whine about," Marcus said through gritted teeth. How many times had Marcus heard those exact words during his childhood? Marcus straightened up, the scowl still firmly etched in his face. "It's time to leave. He's going to keep up his bawling until we get discovered."

"Or we kill him," I added, smiling at my father. *You bring me into this world, and I'll take you out.* I was bluffing, but he wouldn't know that for sure. There was no way I would allow Adriana's fertilized eggs to exist, not after the way she talked about them last night.

Malcolm's eyes widened into saucers. Was he thinking about his sons, the two scientific specimens, both physically superior to him as they discussed his survival? I wanted him to fear for what was about to happen. I wanted my father to pay the price for destroying all of the lives he'd left in the wake of his ambition. His need to prove himself worthy of his father's love. *Shake in your boots, old man.*

"Before we go, I need to ask you something," I said. "Why did you let your alcoholic father's opinion of you dictate your life?"

Malcolm frowned. "Is that what Genevieve told you? Of course she did." He chuckled as if it was an inside joke. "That statement just speaks to her naiveté and how little she knew me or my objectives. This isn't about my father's approval. This is about discovery. The meaning of life. The origin of our species. Doesn't it excite you to know that Adriana's mitochondrial DNA is at its maximum potential? That her chromosomes hold the key to the future of our species?"

"No, it doesn't excite me," I said. "But obviously it gives you a huge hard-on, you sick fuck. And your father. What was his goal when he cloned Adriana's relative? Was this the plan all along? That you'd carry out gene sequencing?"

"You were right about that old man. He was a directionless drunk. He didn't have a goal in mind when he did it. He only did it to see if it could be done." Malcolm stilled and studied my face. "You look like him. Both you and Marcus do. In fact, I think you look more like him than you do me. Phenotype. Keeps the dead alive and brings the past back to haunt you."

I didn't want to hear that I looked like my dead, drunken grandfather who, on a drunken whim, did experiments on people without so much as a second thought.

Adriana jumped into the conversation. "Malcolm, what does the Endosymbiotic theory have to do with me?"

Malcolm smiled. This was obviously the topic he most

loved. "It is a matter of ego, really. Being able to prove the Endosymbiotic theory would allow some people to laud the truth over the others by retrodiction. The previously gathered data on Endosymbiosis is proven by later evidence. You. It will change public acceptance of the theory of evolution. Some scientists, Dr. Bomer in particular, are on a quest to change public opinion, to provide overwhelming evidence to challenge Creationists once and for all. Your DNA is the closest we've come to being able to put the debate to rest."

"Does my DNA prove it then?" Adriana asked.

"You are the living example of the first version, if you will, of the human genome. A living example of the proto-mitochondrial genome. Mitochondria are like cellular power plants, generating most of the cell's chemical energy. The earlier prototype will have the highest levels of chemical energy. Yours happens to be an atavistic mutation to prove all of it true." Malcolm watched Adriana's expression with a look of hope. Was he hoping she'd be impressed and excited to think she was a mutant? He turned to me. "Kalan, you must see how crucial our discoveries are to science, to society, to what we know about human genetics," Malcolm said.

Obviously he was right back at it. I was getting to that point with him where I wasn't sure how much longer I could go without punching him. Part of me wanted to wait and test it out. "I can see that arguing this point with you is about as useful as arguing atheism with a priest, so I'm going to walk away."

"You misunderstand me, Kalan," Malcolm said. "You have at least half your DNA from me and your grandfather. Surely you have some interest in the power of science?"

"Not really, no." I turned to walk away. "It doesn't intrigue me to think about ways I can destroy people's lives and do it for my own benefit, no. I'm also not interested in what you have to say, either."

"I'm sorry about the way we had to retrieve your sample, Kalan." I stopped in my tracks and looked back. Malcolm's expression was a careful attempt to look sympathetic, but it only served to make my blood boil. "But you did have the option your brother chose. Voluntary."

Marcus shrugged, but didn't look pleased. I was well aware of how every set of eyes were fixed on me. My guts soured with realization. Adriana's eggs had probably been fertilized by Marcus's sperm as well as mine.

"I'm afraid the E-jac is unpleasant, and for that, I am sorry, son," Malcolm said.

My face burned and my hands started to shake as humiliation and the horror of that memory hit me like a gale force wind. Adriana's eyes widened. I lost it. I pulled my elbow back and with the speed and power I'd never tapped into before, I slammed my fist into Malcolm's jaw. The crunch of bones vibrated through my knuckles as his head flung backward. Someone in the room gasped. Malcolm's head dangled forward, a massive internal bleed spreading on the left side of his face. His mouth hung open and blood dripped onto his pants.

"You don't know what the word sorry even means," I said through gritted teeth. I grabbed Malcolm by the throat. His eyes were glassy and unfocused. "You will shut your fucking mouth. Do you hear me? I don't want to hear one more fucking word from you."

Malcolm nodded feebly. I let go. The tension in the motel room was unbearable.

All I wanted to do was run. "We need a plan."

*"People should decide for themselves if there is a clear medical advantage, individual benefit or public good, to be found in handing over our entire genome for purposes far beyond our knowledge. In order to do this, more transparency, more public engagement, is vital."*
-Ethics and Genetics

# CHAPTER THIRTEEN

## ADRIANA SINCLAIR

Kalan continued to surprise me. From the mild, self-conscious guy I met a mere few days ago, to this incredibly powerful man he was now, it was hard for my mind to merge the two versions of the same person. He glared down at his father, his posture menacing, his jaw set and his eyes hard and cold as winter ice.

What drove the change home was seeing the way he dealt with Malcolm. Kalan obviously had been far more traumatized than he cared to admit, and the violence he'd unleashed on Malcolm proved it. Part of me was scared at the realization of the magnitude of Kalan's strength and temper, especially because I was certain he was moderating his reaction for us, his audience. The heinous nature of the crime his father orchestrated against him was reprehensible.

Last night Kalan seemed... distracted. It was temporary and fleeting, but now that I knew what happened to him back at the lab, I had to wonder if he was suffering the after-effects of having been violated. Undoubtedly, something like that would affect romance.

The thought of it felt like a hand was inside my chest and squeezing my heart. But I knew Kalan didn't want my pity. That was the last thing he wanted from me. I could see in his face the way he looked after I realized what had happened, that he wished I'd never even found out.

Were my feelings about the situation more about me and my neediness? Here I was, worried about him, when he clearly didn't want or appreciate my concern. Maybe this was about me and my fear of people getting hurt. My fear of losing the people I love.

When I dug deeper, I knew there was one truth I couldn't deny. Despite my desire to shake my insecurity, I couldn't stop how I felt about Kalan any more than I could stop my need for oxygen. An old song popped into my head, my grandmother's favorite. *Oh, love is a many-splendored thing.*

I put it all out of my mind. Right now, with the fierce look in his eye, and the sharp angle of his jaw, he didn't appear to need any sympathy at all.

"I want to get my embryos," I said. "I want them preserved. They're ours, they're our children and we have to protect them, no matter what."

Tait glared at Marcus. "Look what you've done." The blame dripped from his every word. "You brought them to this monster!"

Marcus rolled his eyes. "Hey, I had no idea my old man is an even bigger ass than I am."

Tait let out a disgusted huff of air and turned his back on Marcus. A smile crept across Marcus's face, but there was fleeting emotion that passed through his eyes. An emotion I couldn't place....

Kalan levelled his gaze on Marcus. "What about the eggs?"

Marcus gave Kalan a bored expression, and then picked a piece of lint off his grey shirt. He blinked lazily. "I don't know. Part of me likes the idea of little Adrianas and Marcuses in the world." He winked at me and my lip involuntarily curled back from my teeth. This appeared to amuse Marcus immensely. "But I'm not letting Eros have them."

Kalan was once again nearly vibrating with anger. "Those eggs were taken without her consent, Marcus. Just because you willingly jacked off for your old man doesn't give you the right to control the outcome of what happens to her genetic material."

Marcus burst out in laughter. "You make it sound disgustingly incestuous, brother." He turned to address me. "I suppose we have one goal in common. Neither of us wants Eros to have those eggs. So, we will agree to get them out of there, and then what we do with them will be a matter we can discuss afterward. *If* we pull it off."

The thought of miserable little children that looked partly like me and partly like Marcus flitted through my mind. But I had no other choice. I had to put my trust in Kalan's plan and trust that it would work. It had to work. "Fine."

#

They hauled Malcolm back into Marcus's car, this time, bound and gagged. After Kalan and Marcus argued over whether he should be put into the backseat or the crunched-up trunk, Kalan eventually won the dispute and got his father into the rear seat, right beside him.

I pulled out my cell phone and turned it on. I had fifteen urgent messages. Eight from my mother and the rest from Zoe.

*Where r u?*

*Why r u and Tait not answering??*

*Call me ASAP!*

I typed in her number, and Zoe answered. "Where the hell are you?" she demanded.

"I'm with Tait, Kalan and Marcus. I told her everything in as few words as possible. When I was done, Zoe cursed in my ear.

"We're going back to the lab to get my eggs," I said.

Zoe let out a full shriek that sliced into my eardrum. "No you're not! Get your ass back home and as far away from Marcus and that Malcolm guy as you possibly can. You can add Kalan to that list, too."

"No. I'm not leaving my embryos at a lab. I could never forgive myself for allowing someone to take my children. No."

"They're not children, Adriana," Zoe said, speaking as if she were addressing someone who'd lost touch with reality.

"Not yet."

"I don't think you get it," Zoe said.

Kalan tapped on the window from inside the car to motion it was time to go, and I put an end to Zoe's rant.

"Look. I want you to come here. Just in case. I'm going to call to give you an update before midnight. If I haven't called by midnight, call the cops, okay?"

Another long string of profanities came through the receiver of the phone, but Zoe finally conceded, then said, "This is idiotic. Just for the record." I hung up.

I got in the backseat, beside Kalan who sat in the middle, Malcolm on his right. Marcus drove with Tait in the front passenger seat. Tait was leaning away from Marcus so far that he was practically pressed against the window. But Marcus's posture was relaxed, as if he was oblivious to Tait's disgust. But was he really? Or was it all an act?

Kalan wound his fingers through mine and squeezed. I mouthed the words, "Are you okay?" to him and he nodded, giving my hand another gentle squeeze to accentuate his response.

Beside him, Malcolm watched our entire interaction.

#

We neared the gate at Eros and Kalan's palms were slick with sweat. To his right, Malcolm squirmed and grunted and groaned, his shoulder colliding with Kalan's repeatedly. Kalan gave him a shove. Malcolm grunted again, this time, the grunt sounded a lot like, *I need to talk to you!*

"He wants to talk," Kalan said. "Should I let him talk?"

Through the rear view mirror, Marcus glanced back and shot Malcolm a hostile look. "Let the prick speak."

Kalan untied the gag around Malcolm's head, and his father immediately started talking with a frantic edge to his voice.

"They're going to stop you as soon as we walk in."

Marcus laughed. "Did you think we weren't prepared for that? Come on, I realize you haven't been engineered for superior intelligence, but I assumed you weren't that stupid."

"Then how will you do it?" Malcolm asked.

Marcus glanced back, and observed our father with a half-smile, half-snarl. "You no longer have your fancy weapon to wield against me, do you, Daddy-O?"

"It's not fancy. It's merely a transparent lithium-ion battery. We used silicon lithography, liquid silicone, and electrodes to create an invisible weapon we knew would neutralize your abilities."

This only enraged Marcus further. "I want you to die. I really, really do."

Malcolm stared at his son, his eyes blinking, as if he was

taking in the meaning of the words. Then his eyes closed.

#

Through binoculars, Kalan watched Malcolm pass through the front doors of Eros.

My head was pounding. Kalan's father was under Marcus's mind control, and while Kalan knew it was likely the only possible way they could get the eggs out, I knew it was hard for him to accept Marcus having so much control. The guards were too well prepared to deal with Kalan and Marcus's unique abilities for them to risk going in there with him. But it was obvious Kalan still didn't trust the situation. I could hardly blame him. Too many variables, too many things to go wrong. Not to mention the most troubling underlying problem. We were putting our trust in Marcus not to double cross us.

And Marcus could not be trusted. I'd learned that lesson the hard way.

I sat on the trunk, texting Zoe. Marcus leaned against the car near the headlights, Tait on the other side of the vehicle. The sun beat down on us and Kalan blinked repeatedly. I was certain his eyes were affected by the brightness, one of the major disadvantages to his pale complexion.

Kalan lowered the binoculars when Malcolm disappeared into the mammoth structure. He closed his eyes as if he were praying.

Tait's voice interrupted the silence. "How much of that...

between us... how much of that was real, and how much a manipulation?"

Marcus's eyebrows were high on his forehead as he regarded Tait and his question. "It was all real. And it was all a manipulation. I'm tricky like that."

Tait glared. "That's all you have to say?"

Marcus's whole being screamed indifference.

Tait jumped off of the hood of the car and jabbed his finger into Marcus's chest. "Well, isn't that nice? Is that the only way you can get a piece of ass—to trick people into it?"

Marcus shrugged, noncommittal. "It's not the only way... but it is the easiest. And you have such a pretty ass, Tait."

Tait yelled, "Fuck you!" and pulled his elbow back, his fist hurtling toward Marcus's face. Marcus stopped his fist midair, the two of them struggling, and then Marcus lowered Tait's hand. He held it and pulled Tait into him.

Then Marcus's lips were on Tait's, his hands on either side of his face.

Tait shoved him backward. "Stop it!"

Marcus took a few steps back, laughing. "Your words say stop, but your body says something altogether different—"

"I hate you!" Tait yelled, his eyes red and glossy. "I hate you so much!"

I ran to Tait's side. "Stop it, Marcus!"

"Love and hate are two sides of the same coin, hun."

Marcus's voice was cold.

Tait fisted his own hair in his hands until it stood on end. "Shut up. Shut the fuck up, do you hear me? Leave me alone."

Marcus nodded, his expression bored. "If that's what you want, baby."

"Don't call me that! Don't ever call me that!" Tait had come undone, his eyes wild and bright.

Marcus smiled at Tait and turned away, but not before I caught his eye. There was something in his expression, something I'd never seen before. Something that looked like... regret? Marcus leaned against the driver's side of the car while I hugged Tait.

Kalan spoke to his brother in a low voice. "He's human, you know. He has feelings."

Marcus rolled his eyes at Kalan. "I'm not. Human, that is. He's better off hating me. It'll be easier for him to move on." Marcus made no attempt to lower his voice, and I knew Tait heard every word he said.

Kalan's head tilted to the side. "You love him."

Marcus stared straight ahead, his mouth a hard line. "I don't think I'm capable of that, being that I'm a nonhuman."

"Don't listen to them," I whispered in Tait's ear.

I wanted nothing more than to string Marcus up by the balls. He was a thoughtless, emotionally vacant freak. How he could use someone as sweet as Tait was beyond my understanding. Marcus's colossal flaws were magnified by Kalan's opposite character. The question was—how much of the personality difference was a result of nature, and how much nurture? Was Marcus's horrendous personality something that was genetically engineered? Or did it come about as a result of the impact of life's circumstances? I thought of my embryos, and the possibility that half the genetic material was from Marcus. A shiver slid up my back, even in the sun.

"Maybe if you stopped being such an ass," Kalan said, "and tried to be accountable for your actions, you might be able to make amends—"

"I'm not having this conversation with you," Marcus interrupted. "We are not friends. We are not bros. And I don't need a fucking therapist."

Kalan took a deep breath. "Fine, but you're making a mistake."

Marcus ignored this last comment as he put the binoculars to his eyes and peered at the Eros building. He lowered them and glanced at his watch. "He's been in there for half an hour. If he's not out in fifteen minutes, we need to move on to Plan B."

"What is Plan B?" Kalan asked.

Marcus shot Kalan a contemptuous look. "I don't know, Kalan. You're full of helpful advice today. You tell me."

I steered Tait away and left them to hash it out. We stood at the side of the vehicle, and I grasped his hand. "Hey. I'm sorry about all of this," I said.

Tait took a breath and looked down. "You don't know what it's like, to have feelings for someone, only to find out... He used me."

"I know what it's like when feelings aren't reciprocated. And I know what it's like to be betrayed," I said, inching up beside him so our forearms touched.

He looked at me. "By who?"

I swallowed, my heart staggering in my chest. Was I going to tell him? "Analiese."

Tait's eyes widened. "What? How?"

"Did you know I had a thing for Derek?" I asked. Tait's brow-line furrowed. I continued, "I told her how I felt, that I wanted to date him, and then she..."

"What?" Tait's eyes narrowed, just slightly.

I knew I was on shaky ground. Tait was just as much Analiese's best friend as he was mine. "She deliberately screwed me over and went after him."

Tait's mouth dropped open and he scanned my face. "When? I mean, when did you tell her?"

"I told her a week before she announced they were dating." The image of the two of them, their shadowed silhouettes pressed together in the camper, flashed through my mind once again. I felt like I was inside an iron maiden and all the oxygen from my lungs was forcibly extracted.

Tait shook his head. "She must have misunderstood.

Analiese wouldn't have done that. Not on purpose."

"She did. She knew exactly what she was doing, and she did it to prove a point." My voice was hoarse, my throat full of tears. "That I wasn't better than her. That she could beat me."

"Analiese wasn't like that," Tait said.

"I'm telling you she was." I hesitated. Did I tell him the rest? I'd already said the worst, and now I owed it to myself to have the entire story off my chest, once and for all. "The day she died, something happened... between Derek and me—"

Tait jerked up from leaning on the car and held his hand up between us. "Don't. I don't want to hear it. This isn't about Analiese and her betrayal, it's about you. You can't let go, and you don't know what to do. You're telling yourself lies, so you can let her go. Well, I'm not listening to this bullshit. Not another word, Adriana."

"But I need to tell you the truth!"

Tait shook his head, shoving his hand right into my face. "No! This is bullshit. I'm out. You're on your own," he shouted, right before he took off into a run.

Within thirty seconds he was out of sight. Would he come back?

*New technologies to analyze genetic material are being developed at an unprecedented rate. Indeed, new discoveries may be quickly incorporated into health care practices without sufficient research into their effectiveness or means of delivery. Given the present inability to know the limits or effects of such research, or the context in which genetic information is interpreted and used, caution should be exercised.*
*-National Council on Ethics in Human Research*

## CHAPTER FOURTEEN

### KALAN KANE

Adriana, Marcus and I crept toward the massive concrete fence, coming at it from the side where there would likely be fewer people on guard. We took a metal pole out of the top of a chain-link fence from an adjacent industrial yard. It reached what looked to be about twelve feet, which was more than enough to get over.

We leaned it against the fence, and Marcus went first. When he reached the top, he leaned over and surveyed the grounds surrounding the lab and other outbuildings. He nodded to me and Adriana.

I gestured for Adriana to go next so I could help her up. She scaled the pole with more difficulty but my hands provided a base to push from, and she managed to pull herself up and reach Marcus at the top. He helped her onto the ledge and held her forearm to lower her down to the ground. When she disappeared from my view, Marcus gestured for me to follow.

I was up and over in a flash. Marcus lowered the pole to the other side, and then jumped down. We crouched on the grass beside the retaining wall.

"While we were waiting, I looked up a few things about this building," I said. "This side of Eros is built to meet certain environmental standards. It's more spread out than the other buildings, with more nooks and crannies to use solar panels and for rainwater capture." I pointed to the roof. "Grass is growing on the roof to insulate and keep the heat regulated, but it should also muffle our footsteps. And I'm guessing they don't have motion sensors up there because the grass is always moving, blowing in the wind."

"So we'll go up to the roof to get in?" Adriana asked.

"Yes," I said. "The fans on the top of the building are compact, but the exit ducts on the side are wider because they expel the airflow from the interior. Those exit ducts have vent panels. I'm certain we could easily pop them off."

Marcus's dark gaze raked the building. "And once in, how are we going to know where to get the embryos? And how are we going to keep the guards from taking us into custody?"

"That's your job," I said to Marcus. "Use the element of surprise. What the hell's the advantage of mind control if you don't use it in times like this?"

Marcus smiled. "Right."

I rose from my crouched position and grasped the steel

pole. "Follow me."

I set the pace, Adriana and Marcus on either side of me. I half-carried, half-dragged the steel pole with one end tucked under my arm, the other end scoring the ground behind me. I was hit with a strange feeling. Like someone was right around the corner. I came to an immediate stop and held my hand up for Adriana and Marcus to freeze.

My gut instinct was correct. About two yards away, a guard came into view. I hit the ground and Adriana and Marcus did as well. Thankfully, a water fountain obscured the guard's line of vision and he didn't see us.

Was this intuition? Something deep inside told me something was wrong. This was at least the second time a deep-seated sense that something was about to happen proved correct. I continued on, this time heeding my instincts. I slowed every time I felt it, using the outbuildings to hide, or crouching alongside ornamental trees until they were gone.

We approached one side of the building, and as far as I could tell, there were no guards around. The grey concrete edifice was surrounded by hedges and a sidewalk. Inching closer alongside an outbuilding, I glanced around and closed my eyes to tune into my inner mind. No one was around. I was sure of it.

"We'll climb to the top of the building first, and then we'll pry off that vent there." I pointed to an enormous outer vent only a couple of feet below the roof. Marcus and Adriana nodded in agreement. I hoisted the pole against the side of the building. Marcus held it steady at the top while Adriana kept it stable at the bottom.

This time we had to climb the pole all the way to the top. Marcus went first, his muscles and tendons flexing as he climbed, his shoes tight against the pole at the bottom to thrust him upward. Once Marcus was within two feet of the roof, Adriana shimmied up the pole after him. I helped push her up until she was high above my head, and Marcus grabbed hold of her arm and heaved her onto the roof.

A few moments later, I joined them on the grassy surface.

"Hold my ankles while I lean over and pull that vent lid off," I said. I lay down on my belly, spread out, and with Marcus and Adriana holding my ankles, I grasped the metal pole. I hung over the edge, held on only by the weight of my lower half and their hold on my legs. I managed to grab a side of the metal vent cover where a bolt had come loose. I yanked using brute force, and tore it free. "Okay. I got it."

They dragged me backward until I was once again secure on the roof. I sucked in some ragged breaths, my head pounding from the exertion and the pressure of hanging upside down for so long.

Adriana grasped my hand. "Are you okay?"

"I'm fine." I squeezed her hand and glanced down to survey the grounds below, checking for any signs of trouble. Nothing looked out of place. "All right. Time to crawl."

I wriggled into the ductwork on my elbows and knees. Marcus led, Adriana following behind. At six-foot-two, I felt claustrophobic as hell. Judging by the smell of sweat in the small, contained space, it was likely Adriana and Marcus felt the same way.

For what felt like twenty minutes we wormed our through the ventilation system, the ever-changing airflow adding yet another dimension of annoyance to the process. When the flow increased, my bangs tickled my forehead and poked my eyes, and when it stopped, I dripped sweat. Never in a million years did I think I would dominate the decision-making and planning without so much as a peep from Marcus. Prior to this, Marcus had always run the show, made the decisions, from which hotel to stay at to what route we should take driving. Now I was in charge.

I ran into Adriana's foot when the heel of her shoe swiped my cheek. We came to an abrupt stop.

"I'm at the opening," Marcus whispered. His voice reverberated inside the tin. "There's a hallway, with a guard below. I'll get him under control. Give me a minute."

A moment later, Marcus removed the vent cover. We crawled out into the hallway from above. The armed guard stared straight ahead, unmoving, as if he wasn't even aware of anyone else's presence. Marcus went first, then Adriana, then me. I led us through the room. At the door that turned into the main hall, I stopped and closed my eyes. Then I glanced out into the hallway, and gestured for them to follow.

We entered a sterile, white-on-white hallway and picked up speed. Somehow, I knew where I was going. I'd long ago given up the concept of being able to comprehend the things that were happening when it came to my ever-expanding mutant abilities. It didn't make sense. It never would. Coming to that realization made everything easier.

I came to an abrupt stop, held up my hand in a halt command and peeked around the corner of the hallway.

There were three guards around the bend. Mind to mind, I said, *Three of them*, and held up three fingers. Marcus and Adriana both responded, *Okay*, and a moment later, footsteps rang out, the sound growing smaller, as the person got further away from us.

Marcus grinned that cocky, arrogant smile, white teeth flashing. "Mind control," he whispered. "So much fun."

We took off into a lab with state-of-the-art scientific equipment and gadgets I couldn't possibly identify. I strode directly to the far end of the room toward two closed steel doors. Beside the doors was a nameplate that read, "The Eve Project." Marcus and Adriana were right behind me.

Beyond the steel doors was a refrigerator with five tanks, each one with its own spin-off lid. I opened the first one, and vapour emerged from the top. I reached in and pulled out a cylindrical container and opened it. Six beakers were arranged in a concentric circle inside. I held one up and looked at the fluid. An image flashed through my mind, of children, dark-haired, light-haired, male and female. Was this my imagination? *Jesus, what if it isn't? Stop it.*

Adriana brought a box over, took out one of the cylinders and placed it in the box. I followed suit, and soon, all six cylinders were inside. Without refrigeration, the embryos wouldn't last long, but I knew Adriana wouldn't have it any other way.

The steel doors slammed behind us with a thunderous bang. My eardrums compressed as the interior of the small space filled with enormous pressure. We were plunged into complete blackness

Adriana gasped, "No,"

The cooling system immediately kicked in the moment the door shut. I felt my way to the door, searching for an interior handle.

Adriana's voice was breathless behind me. "Is this a refrigerator or a freezer?"

Marcus answered her. "Freezer."

She cursed under her breath.

I continued to feel along the edge of the door in search of a handle. There was none. I shivered as the temperature dropped several degrees. "There's no handle."

"Fuck." Marcus further accentuated his reaction with what sounded like kicking the wall.

Adriana wrapped her arms around my waist. Wild shudders

wracked her frame. "It's so cold in here. My fingertips are already numb."

Marcus scraped his way to the door. "Now what? We probably have less than an hour before we hit a hypothermic state."

"I don't know... I need to think." My body broke out in an icy sweat as my thoughts spun. Answers evaded me.

I tightened my hold on Adriana to keep her warm, but it didn't help. Within seconds, the temperature dropped several more degrees and now her body quaked from uncontrollable shivers. The tip of my nose tingled and my toes ached.

Marcus kicked the door and a series of knocks responded from outside. Someone was out there.

"Can't you use mind control on them?" I asked.

Marcus's voice was so close to my face I could feel my brother's hot breath on my cheeks. "Obviously not. I have to be in the same room as the person before I can turn them into puppets."

I took a deep breath. There was no point in lashing out at Marcus. Doing so would be useless. Instead, I focused on trying to think of a solution. With each passing moment I grew more aware of my bodily discomfort, and less able to concentrate on finding an answer.

Adriana let go of me and slid down to the ground at my side, her icy hand slipping from my grasp. I sat down beside her and put my arm around her. She was so much smaller than me. It was obvious she was far less able to tolerate the cold than me and

Marcus. Shivers ran up and down my spine, up my scalp. My feet were no longer numb. Now they were burning.

I could hear Adriana's breaths grow increasingly shallow. Every second the temperature dropped, colder and colder. I held her hands in mine. They were ice-cold, as if they were so brittle any pressure would make them snap. I held them to my mouth and blew on them with my hot breath. Them I rubbed them between my palms. It barely helped at all.

"How cold do you think it is now?" I asked.

Marcus spoke, his voice thin and rough, "Most medical freezers are minus forty degrees Celsius."

Think!

"Adriana, are you hanging in?" I asked.

She didn't respond at first and a giant shiver ran through her from head to toe. Then she said, "Yes," through gritted teeth.

I pressed my thumb and forefinger against the bridge of my nose and concentrated on imagining the cooling system of the refrigeration structure. In my minds' eye I saw the coolants boiling on the inside, the pressure building and expanding until they exploded from the heat.

At that moment, the refrigeration door popped open.

A tiny slash of light was visible along the side of the door, and then the door opened wide and Marcus charged out. Three guards flew back from the impact of the door and hit the floor. Marcus focused his intention on them with a menacing glare.

Adriana's lips were blue, and she had dark purple rings below her eyes, her skin blanched white. She blinked at the brightness and then pushed herself off the floor and accepted my hand. I pulled her to standing. We jumped over the pile of guards and ran toward the lab door when the alarm sounded.

Marcus and I ran out, not nearly as affected by the cold as Adriana, who stumbled on her feet. I swept her up into my arms and continued to run at top speed, Marcus and I neck-in-neck. We left the box full of embryos behind.

I skidded around a corner. Shouts emanated from the other end of the long hall. "Distract them," I yelled to Marcus.

Marcus did as he was told, and I watched in amazement as he stealthily moved toward where the voices originated. Yelling broke out, followed by the sound of footsteps and orders shouted by frantic voices.

Adriana and I went toward the ruckus. When I saw Marcus reach the final turn before the lobby, I spoke to him, mind to mind. *"They have the weapon out and are ready for you."* It wasn't something I saw with my eyes, but something I was absolutely certain of, nonetheless.

He turned around, his eyebrows knit together. Then Marcus's expression changed, his eyes flashing. He turned back and pressed himself flush against the wall. Then he leapt out and disappeared from view. I raced after him and rounded the corner in time to see one guard down, Marcus's hands around his neck. A sudden movement caught my eye.

I glanced over. My temple met the tip of a handgun.

Shots rang out and I dropped to my knees. The compression sent a red-hot spike of pain through my ears and my heart momentarily stuttered. Time slowed down, like an old movie reel, sounds overlapping and meshing together. Someone yelled my name. The guard who held the gun to my head made a strange squeak and hit the ground. He clutched his right leg as blood pooled beneath him, his face set in a grimace. I grabbed his gun and stuck it in the waistband of my pants.

Marcus yelled out and twisted the other guard's neck with his bare hands. The man went limp and his body buckled. His knees hit the floor first, followed by his torso. Marcus pulled the weapon from the guard's gun belt and handed it to Adriana.

"Let's blow this place up," Adriana said, her voice calm.

I gaped at her. She'd been so adamant. "But what about all of these people? What about the embryos?"

She shook her head and pointed to the lab right near the front entrance. "Come on." She went in and, without hesitating, turned on a Bunsen burner and snuffed the flame out. She grabbed a latex glove from a box on top of the counter, tied it to the burner, and secured it around the base with another glove as a tie. It slowly began to fill. I watched in amazement as she went to a different burner and turned it on full blast, the flame reaching about a foot into the air.

Then she grabbed my hand and pulled me to the door. "Let's go. I don't know how long we have before this room explodes."

We ran to the entrance of the grand foyer and stopped. I peered around the corner. Oddly, there were few people left in the space, save for five guards who stood shoulder to shoulder, blocking the doorway. They were locked and loaded. Each one had the silicone lithium battery weapon out, ready, and judging by the rabid expressions on all of their faces, they were willing to fight to the end, no matter the outcome.

I whispered, "There are five of them blocking the doors. Their gadgets are out and they look like they want their pound of flesh."

Marcus nodded, his eyes narrowed.

Adriana set her hand on my arm, her palm soft and warm once again. "The silicon thing will only work on you two, right?"

Marcus responded before I could. "Great idea."

"What?" I asked, though I already knew what she was suggesting.

Adriana smiled. "They're not going to kill the Mitochondrial Eve."

My legs grew weak and I grasped her shoulders, staring at her straight in the eye. "No. You can't. I won't let you."

"Kalan." She set her hand on her shoulder, on top of mine. "It has to be this way. You have to let me go. We can't always protect the people we love. We can't always rely on others. Sometimes we have to take the chance and do what has to be done."

I didn't know what to say.

She nodded and shoved the gun into the waistband of her jeans before she stood up on her tiptoes to kiss me. "I have to do this. I realize that now. There are no guarantees in life, and it's scary as hell to do things all on our own, but I love you and I'm going to do this."

She said it out loud. I love you. The lump in my throat felt like a massive rock. I nodded, and my voice came out in a strange croak. "Be careful." She kissed me again, but this time, the kiss was edged with longing. This was possibly the last time we would ever see each other. When Marcus cleared his throat, she pulled away from me. My chest ached, as if my heart might explode into a million pieces.

She gave a cursive nod to Marcus, and without hesitation, walked directly into the lobby, her hands over her head.

*"Rare genetic variants are indeed very important..."*
*-TerraDaily.com*

## CHAPTER FIFTEEN

### ADRIANA SINCLAIR

As soon as I stepped out in front of the guards, every gun and every silicon weapon was aimed directly at me. My heart pounded so loud in my ears everything sounded like it was filtered through water.

"Do. Not. Move!" One of the guards shouted. The others were stock-still, their eyes and guns on their target. Me.

*This is it.* I put my hands up, but they didn't move an inch. Would they shoot me? Or was this just an intimidation strategy? Surely Malcolm would have notified all of his staff about my importance? Staring down the barrels of those massive black guns made me seriously question my assumption. But what other way was there? I either got us out now, or we would be captured and possibly tortured further. I couldn't let that happen. I sucked in a deep breath. *Just do it.*

Using every ounce of inner fortitude, I placed one foot in front of the other. The action startled them, and several of the guards shuffled on their feet, their hands trembling as they steadied their aim. Shouting erupted from them all, simultaneously.

I ignored it. I ignored the pounding in my head, the ringing in my ears. *Keep walking. Death will be quick. It shouldn't hurt much. Analiese is gone. My future children are about to be destroyed. If I don't do this we'll all be captured anyway. There is nothing left to lose and everything to gain.*

I lowered my arms and dropped them to my sides. There was no use in pretending. I wasn't surrendering. Instead, I smiled and shrugged at the guards. Their bodies stiffened, and seeing their reaction gave me a strange sense of power, a feeling of complete and utter immunity. I had their attention now. I had control of the entire room and they all knew it.

Knowing Kalan would be freaking out back there, I sent him a thought. *I'm okay.*

Most of the guards continually glanced toward the centre guard, and I assumed he was their leader. I walked directly toward him with stealth. I felt like a lioness, stalking my prey. Queen of the jungle.

"Stop moving. Right now!" he yelled.

I shook my head and continued on. Slow and steady. "No." I smiled.

"Miss, if you don't stop, we will have to make you stop. One way or another," the head guard said. His eyes were hard as flint, his black goatee giving him a fierce countenance.

There was nothing they could do to intimidate me at this point. "You won't do anything to risk your paycheck. You know I'm the Mitochondrial Eve."

His eyes narrowed as he hesitated. "Not another step. I mean it."

I chuckled. "I think you might be interested in knowing the risk you and your men are facing at this moment." My comment elicited a furrowing of his brow. "I have set the lab on fire. And I think you know what that means."

Every head jerked toward their leader. He stared straight at me, his eyes wide. He blinked. "Go!" he yelled.

Simultaneously, every gun was lowered and the armour-clad men scrambled toward the exit. They were gone in moments.

I turned back. "Let's go!" I yelled. Kalan and Marcus came out from around the corner and we went straight for an alternate exit. Once out of the building, we ran full tilt. I was slower, so Marcus helped Kalan grasp me under the arms, the two of them almost lifting me off my feet. I felt like I was in an animated film. The roadrunner, my legs going round and round. I pushed my aching bones and barely thawed muscles and ran as hard as I could, my breathing ragged. Marcus let go.

A thunderous boom rang out from behind. We were blasted forward, forced onto our hands and knees, onto bare pavement. Stabbing pain exploded through my knee and palms where I came into contact with concrete and I cried out. Dust, thick and grey, swirled around us as particulate rained down and pelted our backs. Kalan covered his mouth, as did I, but the effort was useless, the air was so thick with the fine dust.

Kalan scrabbled to his feet and grasped my arm. My body was wracked with great gasping coughs and Kalan hacked as well. *I'm going to die. In the end, we are all alone.* My mother's face flashed through my mind. I couldn't leave her. I started to run.

"Marcus! Take her other arm!" Kalan yelled. "She's not going to survive if we don't get her out of here."

I couldn't see him, but I knew Marcus was with me when the weight on my feet lifted. We ran. This time I forced my legs to move, my body taxed beyond anything I'd ever experienced before.

Eventually, the particles in the air thinned out, but I continued to cough. Once within a block of the car, Kalan picked me up and ran with me in his arms. I coughed and sputtered, my body curled forward as coughs morphed into gagging.

Tait already had the back door of the car open, his eyes wide as we approached. Kalan lowered me into the backseat and got in beside me. I slumped over onto him and coughed and hacked so hard Kalan's t-shirt was speckled with a thin spray of blood.

"Go!" Kalan yelled.

With a screech of tires, Marcus peeled away. The wail of sirens echoed in the distance.

*No longer will a child be considered a blessing from God, but rather, a product manufactured by a scientist. Man will be a created being of man.*
*-All About Popular Issues*

## CHAPTER SIXTEEN

### KALAN KANE

I'd never seen Marcus drive so fast. We weren't being pursued, but he continued to speed along, weaving in and out of traffic like a professional racer. But it wasn't nearly fast enough.

Adriana's face had turned a deathly white. Her lips and under her nose were dry and chalky with dust from the blast. Her wracking coughs finally stopped, but now she was unconscious. There was no comfort in the quiet, only a deep sense of dread. At least when she was coughing, so hard she had to hold her side, her eyes streaming tears of pain, she'd been conscious. At least I'd known she was still... alive. Now? *God, if you do exist, I really need you. Please.*

"Adriana, stay with me," I whispered as I held her clammy face to mine. She was floppy as a rag doll, her body heavy in its slack state.

Tait whimpered in the front passenger seat. Obviously, he'd

had a change of heart about walking away from Adriana in her time of vulnerability. "Oh, God," Tait's voice wavered. "Why did I say that to her? Why didn't I come to help you? I'm so sorry." He pressed the back of his shaking hand against his mouth and continually glanced back at Adriana with red-rimmed eyes.

Marcus spoke to Tait, his voice gentle and supportive. "Blaming yourself isn't going to help her now."

Tait ignored Marcus. "Kalan. Is she going to be okay?" he asked. Before I could respond he turned to Marcus and yelled, "Hurry up! Drive faster!"

"This is as fast as the car goes," Marcus said perfunctorily. No snide remarks. No quick comeback. Was this the real Marcus?

Tait leaned back and pressed his hand to her forehead. He jerked his hand back, and his eyes widened. I knew he'd felt her cold, clammy skin.

"What if she doesn't...?" Tait's voice was barely a whisper. He shook his head and squeezed his eyes shut and pressed his hand over his mouth once again.

Adriana convulsed in my arms. Her eyes rolled back in her head and her mouth dropped open, a strange choking sound emerging from her throat. I shuffled aside so I could lay her down on the backseat. I hovered over her, my ear to her mouth. There was no sound. "Oh, God! No. Please. Please!" I pressed my fingers to her neck. There was no pulse. My heart fell through to my knees.

I started chest compressions.

In some faraway part of my mind I heard Tait's hysterical questions, but I couldn't answer. I could only hear my ragged breaths and my own pulse thundering through my ears. I couldn't take the energy to respond. I had to restart her heart.

After twenty compressions, I leaned over her mouth and listened. Still nothing. Tait continued to badger me with shrill questions I ignored. Adriana's lips were blue, her skin tone like ash. I repeated another twenty compressions and listened. Nothing.

"Adriana!" I yelled. Marcus swerved to the side of the road and slowed. I punched the back of his seat. "Keep fucking driving! We need to get her to a hospital!" I did another round of compressions, my head pounding, my ears ringing. My own heart rate kept pace with every up and down motion I made. Fifteen. Sixteen. My wrists ached. Seventeen. Eighteen—

Something snapped beneath my fingers, a crunch that vibrated up my palm and made a shiver crawl up my spine.

I'd broken her ribs.

I hesitated, my hands shaking. Another strange sound came from my throat. A gurgle. "Adriana! No. No!" I looked around the car, and took in the horrified expressions of Tait and Marcus. I looked back down to her. Beneath her eyes were dark purple hollows, magnifying her bluish lips. "Oh, God! What should I do?" I placed my hands back on her chest, but I couldn't bear to press down again. What if the broken rib punctured her heart? It would kill her. But if I stopped compressions, she was dead anyways.

I no longer had an ounce of strength. "I'm so sorry." I put my hands over her chest and leaned over her so I could use my body weight. Tears fell from my eyes and rained all of her face. One fell into her right eye. I started compressions once again. One. Two. Three.

Instantaneously, the skin around her eye returned to its normal colour. Was I having some kind of delusion? Was I seeing what I wanted to see?

"Oh my God! Kalan, look!" Tait said from the front seat.

Her mouth closed and then opened, and she sucked in a noisy breath. She wheezed so loudly her breath crackled.

A strange tightening built inside my chest followed by pressure in my eyes. Tears slid from my cheeks as I watched her eyes close and then flutter open, the teal irises visible once again.

With each of my tears that fell on her skin, something changed. First, her complexion changed from chalky to rosy once again. The dark circles beneath her eyes disappeared. Then, her breathing evened out. How was this happening? Were my tears doing this?

"What's happening, Kalan?" Tait demanded.

"She's healing," I said.

#

The emergency room admitting staff were as brusque and unfriendly as usual. They wanted the facts, and with each detail we shared, the deeper the furrows in their brows.

"She was near a building when it exploded," I repeated for the third time. At least this time, it was the police and not hospital personnel staring at me like I had two heads.

"And you weren't there?" The grey-haired cop asked. He had heavy circles under his eyes and deep grooves on either side of his mouth. It looked like he hadn't slept in years.

"That's what I said, yes."

"So how, exactly, did you know she was there?" He wrote in his notebook quickly and went back to scrutinizing my face.

"She called me on her cell and told me where she was. I found her in the parking lot," I held his gaze with what I hoped looked like wholesome confidence.

"Why was she near the Eros lab?" he asked. His hand was still on his notepad as he awaited my response. His gaze felt like it drilled a hole into me.

"She was out for a run. She's training for a half-marathon."

He peered at me in silence. His eye twitched. Then he started writing again. "Strange area to train in. Not exactly a residential area. And you two aren't even from Denver."

"Adriana runs ten and fifteen miles at a time. She covers a lot of ground. I'm sure she didn't start out there." I was thinking on my feet, hoping it all made sense. "We were in Denver on a day trip."

"Why?"

"Something to do."

His eyes narrowed. "Where did she start her run, then?"

My mind whirred. Where was the car? What was a plausible reason for her to have run that far?"

Marcus came up behind me, patted me on the back, and smiled at the police officer.

"Adriana asked me to drop her off a few blocks from there. She was planning to stop in at Eros to see if they could help her understand her blood disorder," Marcus said, his demeanor calm and relaxed. "She was trying to find a geneticist who would have some insight into her and her sister's genetic condition."

Adriana's beautiful face drifted into my mind. She was so courageous, having gone through what she had. The death of her sister, such a short time ago, getting kidnapped, and then coming up with a strategy to evade the guards and blow the building. I had nothing but the utmost respect for her.

The police officer's gruff voice pulled me from my inner thoughts. "Who are you?" he asked, his eyes flicked back and forth between us.

"He's my twin," I said. Marcus flashed a fake smile.

The police officer grunted in acknowledgement. "What's this about her sister's case?"

"Adriana has a blood disorder. Her sister died a few weeks ago," Marcus made a face, an attempt at looking concerned. "Botched blood transfusion."

Now the cop's grey eyebrows met in the middle. "And this Eros place, what is it?"

Marcus set his hand on the cop's shoulder. He looked at Marcus's hand like it was contaminated.

Marcus levelled his gaze at the police officer. "Look. My brother is concerned about his girlfriend. Might I suggest you ask me the questions, and let him check on Adriana?"

The police officer's pupils dilated and his face drooped. Marcus smiled. "Problem solved."

"Hardly. He'll still have to put in his report. It's going to look pretty incomplete."

"I'll deal with him later." Marcus shrugged. "You should go to Adriana. She'll be gaining consciousness soon."

"Where's Tait?" I asked.

"He's getting us coffee."

I cocked my head to the side. "On his own free will?" I asked.

"Funny." Marcus glared in response. "What happened? She was dying. I've never heard of anyone enduring so many compressions and then miraculously coming back to life. What did you do?"

"My tears. They healed her," I said. Just saying it sounded preposterous.

Marcus smiled and nodded as if his suspicions had been confirmed. "I knew it." He started laughing, his laughter oddly happy and out of place. "Jesus. The three of us are fucking freaks."

"So you've never done that... I mean, healed someone before?" I asked.

Marcus's face twisted in a look of mocking. "Are you kidding? Do you think I've ever cried over anyone in my entire life?"

He had a point. Did people like Marcus cry about anything?

"What about Genevieve?" I asked.

"What about her?" Marcus's expression was unreadable.

"She must have died in the explosion," I said. Finding her and then losing her in such a short period of time hurt. Even though we'd communicated only a few words to one another, most of it mind to mind, I'd found her to be a lovely person. Someone I wanted to know better, someone who could have finally unlocked the secrets to my existence. I knew some details, through observing conversations between her and Malcolm, but there was so much more I'd wanted to ask her. And now I never could. Forever an orphan.

I watched Marcus, unable to predict his response. He'd endeared himself to me in the last few hours and I hoped it would continue.

"Screw her. She deserved what she got." Marcus spun on his heel and walked away.

My hope evaporated.

*"I see no conflict in what the Bible tells me about God and what science tells me about nature."*
*-Francis Collins, Director, National Human Genome Research Institute*

## CHAPTER SEVENTEEN

### ADRIANA SINCLAIR

I awoke to Mom hovering over me, her eyes glassy and bloodshot. I glanced around. Everything in the room was ivory and off-white, from the walls, to the curtains, to Mom's complexion. I was in the hospital.

She caressed my cheek with her thumb. "Hi."

"Hi," I said with a croak. My throat felt raw and hot, like I'd swallowed sandpaper and then sucked on a banana pepper.

"You're in the hospital," Mom said, a tear dripping down her cheek and over her chin.

"I guessed that much."

"Your friend, Kalan, told me what happened," she said. "What I don't understand is why you would be jogging in that area in the first place?"

I wasn't ready for this discussion. Not yet. "I don't

remember much. Honestly."

She let out a breath. "Of course you wouldn't remember. We can talk about that later. I'm so happy you're okay. I couldn't bear the thought of losing you too…" The last words came out in a whisper.

"I know. I'm sorry."

She held my hand to her face. Her skin was surprisingly cold and clammy. "The doctor says you're just fine."

I tried to smile. I had so many things to say to her, and small talk was only getting in the way. I squeezed her hand. "Mom, can I ask you something?"

"Of course. Anything."

"I went to visit Uncle Les. At his house."

My mom stared at me in complete silence for several moments, before finally, she spoke.

"Why would you go there, Adriana?" Mom's words were slow. Too slow. She was trying to maintain her calm, I knew it. "I told you to stay away from him."

"He said something," I paused. How does a person say something like this, out loud?

Another drawn-out silence. Then, "What? He told you what?"

"He made it sound like he is…" I couldn't bring myself to say the word. It was just all wrong. "He inferred that he is my… me and Analiese's… our father." The moment I said it I felt like throwing up.

"What?" My mother's voice had turned into an icy whisper. "That godamn liar—"

"Is it true? Did he abuse you?"

She stared at me with eyes that flashed white. "Tell me you are not going to listen to a single word that dirty old man said. Please. Tell me you aren't going to listen to it," Mom said, her voice pitchy and winded. "Will you promise me that, Adriana? Will you?"

"I'll forget about it. If you say I should ignore what he said, I will. I promise." Did I believe what I was saying? Could I really ignore what he said and forget all about it? Something in my gut, a strange twisting feeling, told me I wasn't going to forget about it anytime soon.

"Good." Her eyes continued to dart around, as if she was searching for something to change the subject. She smiled. "Kalan and Marcus aren't nearly as scary as what Grandma and Aunt Bethany made them sound, are they?"

*If you only knew how scary they really were.* "No. They're just regular guys. Well, sort of."

"Fraternal twins, then?" She didn't wait for me to confirm, "They look so much alike, if it wasn't for their coloring, I'd swear they were identical."

Not much point in trying to explain the truth. "Yeah. Fraternal."

"They're nice boys. The pale one, Kalan, sure seems to have taken an interest in your well-being. I almost think he has a crush on you."

A crush didn't even come close to describing how we felt about each other. "Really? I don't know about that."

"Well, speak of the devil!" Mom said. I followed her gaze to the doorway of the hospital room where Kalan stood, a strange expression on his face.

"Hi," I said.

Kalan smiled at my mom and then closed the space between us with a few long, purposeful steps. He sucked in a long, audible breath. "How are you feeling?"

"I'm okay."

Mom's shuffled on her feet and let out an awkward cough. "I'll leave you two to talk. I'll come back in a few minutes, okay, Adriana?"

"Sure." She left the room, looking at us out of the corner of her eye. How much did she know?

When she was gone, I reached up and ran a fingertip over Kalan's lips. "How are you feeling?"

Kalan kissed my forehead. "One-hundred percent. The benefit of rapid healing."

I tried to raise my head and look down at my body, but my neck was too stiff. "Is there anything wrong with me?"

Kalan shook his head. His chest heaved with yet another

long intake of air. "A broken rib that now appears like just a fracture. Some bumps and bruises. You inhaled a lot of dust..."

"A broken rib?" I tried to recall a moment where I'd broken a rib, but I couldn't. "How did that happen?"

Kalan's expression drooped. Guilt? The man wore his heart on his sleeve. "It's my fault. I was doing chest compressions, and... I broke your rib. I'm so sorry."

Chest compressions? The last thing I remembered was running. "Why were you doing chest compressions?"

"You had no pulse. You inhaled too much dust." Kalan looked like he was confessing to a murder. "But the doctors say your healing rate is faster than normal."

"Faster than normal?" I asked. "Why?"

Kalan once again had an odd expression on his face. One I couldn't read at all. He pursed his lips together and then answered, "I thought I'd lost you. I'd been doing compressions for so long... and then I broke your rib on top of it. I... I was sure it was over." His voice broke, and he completed his words in a near-whisper. "One of my tears fell into your eye, and then everything changed. You started to heal."

"The tears? Mine burn you and yours heal me?" I could hardly believe it.

Kalan nodded. "Apparently, yes."

I shook my head. How was this possible? What more could Kalan do that we didn't know about? What more could I do? My tears burned him, but why? Was it the Endosymbiotic theory at work? Malcolm's words flitted through my mind, *"Mitochondria are like cellular power plants, generating most of the cell's chemical energy. The earlier prototype will have the highest levels of chemical energy. Yours happens to be an atavistic mutation to prove all of it true."*

"Thank you." I grabbed his hand and squeezed.

His Adam's apple bobbed in his throat and he blinked rapidly, his eyes glassy. "You're welcome." He smiled and his entire demeanor changed. "Anytime."

"There are so many unanswered questions. Are we ever going to get answers?" I asked. It was a rhetorical question, but it had to be raised.

"I don't know. Probably not."

I lifted my head to glance around the room. My neck was stiff and tender. The room was empty. "What about Eros? Was it on the news?"

Kalan nodded. "No survivors. They're investigating foul play. But so far, they're saying it looks like 'human error.'"

My neck gave way and my head flopped down on the pillow. "Where's Marcus?"

"He's fine. He's here, somewhere."

I stared at Kalan, to see if he was joking. Marcus stayed at the hospital? For me?

"Where's Tait?" I asked.

A voice behind Kalan answered. "I'm right here." Tait stepped into the room and went around the other side of my bed. He sat down beside me and grasped my hand. He squeezed it, a little too hard. "I didn't mean the things I said. You know that, right?" Tait asked.

"I think you meant it at the time," I said.

Tait shook his head, his mouth turned down at the corners. "No, I didn't. I was angry. Angry at Marcus, for the way he used me. Angry at myself for getting used that way. And angry at you, for constantly holding a mirror up in front of me so I had to face who I was. I didn't want to face the truth about myself, and I wanted someone else to share in the humiliation and self-loathing I had at that moment. I was looking for an excuse to lash out at someone, and you just happened to be the person on the receiving end of it. I'm sorry."

"It didn't take much to make my self-loathing kick in," I said. "In fact, the self-loathing has been there every day, every second, every moment since I got the phone call that Analiese was in the hospital."

"Adriana, you did nothing wrong," Tait said. His eyes filled with moisture. "Analiese had her problems. She wasn't always the best sister, and you weren't either. None of us are perfect."

I choked up.

"Will you accept my apology? For abandoning you at the worst possible moment? For being a horrible friend? For taking my pain out on my most loyal, trusted friend? Please, forgive me, Adriana. I'm an ass."

I chuckled, a strange sound mixed with a sob. "You're forgiven, dummy." I ruffled his hair. "Now stop looking at me like that. Or I'm going to start bawling, and I don't want to do that. Did you know I have killer tears?"

"Thank you." Tait looked like he was barely containing his own tears. He glanced back at the door. "Look who else is here, lurking around." Tait moved aside and Zoe came into view. She rushed to my bed.

Zoe grabbed my hand and squeezed it, hard. "I came when you called, like you asked."

"Thanks."

Zoe peppered me with questions about how I was feeling, sometimes the same question over and over in that motherly way, as if she wasn't convinced I felt as well as I claimed. To prove my point, I sat upright in the bed. It hurt like hell. Maybe it wasn't just to prove it to her.

"There. Satisfied?" I asked. She smiled and rolled her eyes.

Tait's eyes twinkled. "This is cause for celebration!" He held his hands above his head and spoke in a shrill, nasal tone, one of his many movie voices he liked to imitate. It had a very Dorothy from The Wizard of Oz sound to it.

"As soon as party girl is ready," Zoe said in the same high, nasal tone. She did jazz hands for effect.

I smiled, but somehow, I didn't think I'd be ready for the party scene for a while. Marcus walked through the door, and it was as if his presence cast a dark cloud over the room. He carried two coffees, one for himself, and one for Kalan. He handed Kalan his coffee.

"Welcome back to the world of the living," Marcus said.

Tait stared at him, blue eyes intense, jaw set. "That's my cue to leave."

Marcus turned his head to the side, his gaze impenetrable. "Whatever you need, sugar."

Tait's nostrils flared and his face flushed hot pink. He didn't respond, opting to turn his back on Marcus and leave the room. Zoe followed behind him.

Marcus rolled his eyes and walked around to where Tait had stood moments before. "How's our special girl?" he asked. How did Marcus manage to look and sound cocky no matter what he did?

"Marcus, why are you so mean to Tait?" I asked, straight to the point. "He's obviously in love with you, and yet, you can hardly bring yourself to be polite."

"Of course he's in love with me." Marcus took a gulp of his coffee. "I'm just adorable that way, I guess."

I scowled.

Marcus laughed. "What? I speak the truth."

Kalan shook his head. "Maybe you shouldn't speak. You're

moderately more tolerable that way."

I grasped Marcus's chin and pulled him down to me. Face-to-face. I stared him straight in the eye and spoke in a hushed tone, my fingers firm on his jaw. "I know you love him. Stop being such a jerk."

Marcus placed his hand on my shoulder and moved in to me so our faces were barely an inch apart. His eyes were hard and imperious. "I am not capable of love, Adriana. Please get that through your head because I'm not going to say it again." His jaw muscle twitched as he waited for a counterchallenge. I didn't respond.

Kalan came around to Marcus's side of the bed and his presence alone spoke volumes. Marcus stood upright and flashed us a big, fake smile. "See you two kids later."

With his typical arrogant swagger, Marcus strode out of the room. The dark cloud lifted.

"Do you know what I've learned from Marcus?" I asked.

Kalan mouth twisted into a wry smile. "What? That people are selfish and unpredictable? That they can be your enemy one minute and your ally the next, if it serves their purpose? I can't imagine you've learned anything of value."

"I've learned there are no truly evil people," I said. "The things we experience, the trauma and pain, it changes us, breaks us, irreparably. It's the environment that causes us to behave poorly."

Kalan's eyebrows rose. "Poor behavior barely covers the enigma that is Marcus. What about Malcolm? He's evil personified."

I shook my head, and pain speared up through my neck. "Malcolm is an example of insecurity, indifference and ambition, all combined to make a person immune to the idea of morality. He's not so much evil. He just has a complete lack of concern for anyone or anything other than his preoccupation," I said. "His indifference keeps him safe, because he doesn't have anyone in his life to worry about or to lose. But it keeps him from connecting with people. People like Genevieve. It keeps him utterly alone."

Kalan chewed on his bottom lip. "So the question is, was he born indifferent or did that part of him develop as a result of circumstances, being around a distant, alcoholic father who never approved?"

"I would venture a guess that it was the circumstances in his life," I said. "Have you ever met a child who didn't respond to love and encouragement? Marcus's need to push people away is also because of his trauma. He was rejected by your mother, and abused by his adoptive parents," I said. "We can ask ourselves, would you or I be any different under those circumstances?"

"Personality plays a part, too. Not everyone with mommy issues turns out to be a freak like Marcus," Kalan said.

"True. But doesn't at least the foundation of our personality come from our genes? And don't you and Marcus have the exact same genes?" I asked.

Kalan chuckled. "You're good. Did you study the Socratic Method, or what?"

I smiled. "Of course. That was back in the days when I was thinking about going into Law School."

"Oh, Christ. I'd hate to be cross-examined by you," Kalan said. "I'd get mesmerized by your beauty and then forget everything I was going to say."

"I would have made a terrible lawyer. But guess what? I think I finally know my major."

His brow quirked. "Oh?"

"I want to know if there are more of us out there, like me, Analiese, your mother and you. And I want to fully understand my mitochondria and its implications. I've decided I want to go into Genetic Sequencing," I said.

"Isn't it a little too close to home?" Kalan asked.

I shrugged. "I don't know. After all we've been through I can't imagine that studying anything else would hold any interest for me."

"I can see why." Kalan paused, and then opened his mouth again as if he was going to say something. Instead, he closed it.

"What is it?" I asked.

His lips pursed together. "You know the embryos are gone, right?"

I nodded as I felt the familiar stinging in the back of my

eyes. It was stupid. "They were never meant to be. I realize that now. They weren't real people, and my trying to preserve them... It wasn't about the embryos at all."

"What was it about?"

I swallowed. "Keeping the embryos alive won't bring Analiese back."

Kalan's lips flattened, pressed together. "You're right. I'm so sorry you lost her, Adriana. There was unfinished business between the two of you."

I blinked back tears. "Isn't that the problem with life? Or, more accurately, death? We'll always have unfinished business, things we've said, or didn't say. Things we've done, regrets that will haunt us."

"I never got to know my mother at all," Kalan said. "There were so many things I wanted to say to her. So many things I wanted to ask. Now, I'll never get to."

I squeezed his hand. "Maybe one day you will?"

His head jerked to look at me. "You still believe in Heaven, after all you've learned, all you know about genetics?"

"If we don't have Heaven, what do we have? A dirt hole? Worms to turn us back into dirt?" I shook my head. "I can't accept that."

"So this is about hope and faith?" Kalan asked. He eyed me with a strange kind of intensity.

"In the end, hope and faith is all we've got," I said.

"Wow." He pushed a stray hair from my face. "I never would have predicted that following the decision to go into genetic sequencing you'd make a declaration of religious belief."

"I'm full of surprises, Kalan. Just wait." I stroked the growth on Kalan's jaw and savoured the downy softness. "There's another contradiction I've come to grips with."

"Oh?"

"Yes." I hesitated. "I have realized through all of this that I need people. I spent my whole life wanting independence, to not need Analiese. When she died, I was lost, directionless. I couldn't face life without the one person I'd spent nearly every day with, the person who was part of me. I realized then, it was a gift. We were created as one, and even though we'd split apart in utero, we were both one-half of the other. I couldn't let her go. I couldn't face life without her by my side. I raged against both my need for independence and my weak, crippling need to depend on her."

"You are independent, Adriana. Look at what you've been through. If you were a weak, dependent person, you never would have gotten through it all."

Tears built up in my eyes once again. I didn't fight them. "But don't you understand? It's not about that. I can have it both ways."

"I don't get it," Kalan said.

I giggled, a strange choking sound from the tears gathered in the back of my throat. "I need people. I need to lean on others as much as I need to be able to stand on my own two feet. There's no requirement in the rulebook of life that says we must be able to withstand life's pressures and pain by ourselves. This is what I've come to understand. I'm allowed to need other people, for my survival, and it's not some kind of weakness or flaw. It's human nature. Just like our need to rely on the idea of Heaven, despite not having any evidence to prove its existence."

"That can be part of our LifeMapApp. A self-actualization component. If the user realizes they can be both independent and dependent on others for love and support, the hurdles of life are easier to overcome," Kalan smiled. "I'm happy you've figured this out—"

"Kalan," I interrupted, "What I'm trying to say is... I need you. I need you, more than I wanted to admit out loud. But after everything that has happened, I don't care anymore. Life's too short to deny our true feelings. I need you so much, it hurts."

Kalan's whole frame slumped forward, and he gently laid his head on my chest. "I can hear your heartbeat."

"Aren't you going to say anything?" Heat built up in my cheeks.

Kalan pulled back to look at me, his eyes glossy. "I don't know what to say. That my heart is beating so fast right now I feel like it's going to jump out of my chest? That I feel like running around this room and screaming at the top of my lungs? Words don't describe what I feel right now."

I looked up at him. "Try."

"I don't know what to do, how to deal with these feelings. We're related. What does that mean for us? I've spent the majority of my life thinking only sick, banjo-playing hillbillies were incestuous. People who grew up in the sticks and never left. But now, I'm in love with my relative. Now I'm one of those banjo-playing hillbillies."

If he didn't look so dejected, I would have chuckled. "We're not brother and sister. We're what—second or third cousins?"

He shrugged, his shoulders curled. "Does it matter? We're still related." Kalan yodeled the dueling banjo riff from the movie Deliverance. "It's sick. Isn't it?"

It was a legitimate question, not a rhetorical one. "Says who? God? That's where most incest laws come from, the Bible. But I think we know those Biblical rules were a way to prevent people from marrying and having babies and passing along hereditary diseases. Clearly Malcolm has no such concerns. Hell, that was his master plan all along. Consanguineous."

Kalan's eyes narrowed. "I can't even hear that man's name without wanting to punch the wall."

I grabbed his hand, which was shaking. "Under normal circumstance, incest is wrong. But we aren't in this world because of normal circumstances. We've never met before. We're distantly related. And if there is a question of abnormal children, there are ways to prevent that aren't there?"

"You'd give up having children to be with me?" Kalan didn't blink as he waited for my response.

I brought his hand to my lips and kissed his fingers. "I would give up a lot for you. You can't even imagine how much I'd give up, just to be with you."

Kalan closed his eyes, his head dropping down to my chest once again. "Oh, God. How did I get so lucky?"

I kissed the top of his head this time, the scent of hair like cedar and musk mixed together. "I'm the lucky one."

"Adriana, you are my life. All I've ever wanted was a family, people to validate me, confirm that I'm real, that I belong. But what I've come to realize is that blood isn't what binds people together. It's love. It's sounds cliché and hokey, I know, but I don't care." Kalan blinked rapidly. "You are my family now."

"Now I'm speechless," I said.

Kalan lay down beside me and snuggled in so we were face-to-face. I suddenly wondered what I looked like to him right now, horizontal, in a hospital bed, a white hospital gown on, white hospital sheets. The image of Adriana's cold, white body flashed through my mind.

I pushed thoughts of Analiese to the back of my consciousness, and focused back on the here and now, on Kalan, on life.

He stroked my hair from my head all the way down my back. A shiver ran through me. He pressed his lips to mine. It was a gentle, chaste kiss and all the oxygen left my lungs. I craved more. When Kalan moved away, I pulled him back to me.

"We're in a hospital here," Kalan's voice vibrated through my lips.

"Does it look like I care?" I smiled and wrapped my arms around his waist.

"Not really." Kalan kissed me again.

If you enjoyed this book, keep up on all my latest book news by joining my Mailing List at joannebrothwell.com. List members receive advanced notice on latest releases, events and my newsletter, as well as exclusive access to The Marcus and Tait Chronicles, a series of deleted love scenes between the lovers! And don't worry, your e-mail address will never be shared!

Visit my author page on Facebook (Author Joanne Brothwell) to keep up with my writerly shenanigans.

And feel free to check out my fiction books, also on Amazon Kindle:

The Stealing Breath Series:

**Stealing Breath**

Beware those with the Stealing Breath...

**Silencing Breath**

Will Sarah succeed in rescuing Evan from the Malandanti?

A Twisted Fairy Tale:

**Forest of the Forsaken: The Witch's Snare**

An eerie adult twist on Hansel and Gretel.

# Acknowledgements

I would like to thank my husband and my children, who patiently listen to the problems of my fictional people. I'd like to give a special thank you to my brainiac big brother, Dr. Doug Brothwell, for helping me piece together science that is way over my head. Thanks to Joanne, Tanjia and Dorothy for giving me insight into what an emergency room situation would look (and smell) like. To Karyn Good, Diane Rinella, Rebecca Florizone, Jefferson Smith and Heather Sowalla who agreed to take a look at an earlier draft and were polite enough not to crush my self-esteem. To Karen Rought, for lightning-fast editing. To Darren, for the final round of line edits as you burned the candle at both ends. To Ravven, for her stunningly gorgeous cover art. I have never seen another cover that comes even close.

And most of all, I'd like to thank my readers. You are loyal, and I am so happy you took a chance on me and purchased my work. Thank you!

## JOANNE BROTHWELL

JOANNE BROTHWELL lives in the country on the Canadian prairie with her family where her stories are inspired by the dead things that appear at her doorstep on a daily basis.

You can find her online at www.joannebrothwell.com

Made in the USA
Middletown, DE
13 October 2023

40745176R00166